A PERFECT LIKENESS

RENEE KIRA

First Edition

Published June 2020

Published by Renee Kira Books

reneekirabooks.com

Title: A Perfect Likeness / Renee Kira (author)

ISBN: 9780648868507

1

ISOBEL

Something about this coastline leads people to bad outcomes. I can't remember a summer since my childhood that passed without a death. Usually, it's the water that kills. A surfer who showed no concern to the jagged outcrops, or a swimmer tugged down by a rip. Last year, a tourist got knocked off a low rocky shelf by a rogue wave and was never seen again.

The weather changes fast on the coast; the sky and the sea tell me more than any forecast. Each morning, I spend a minute or two watching the horizon before I leave home.

Today I watch while I sip my coffee, leaning against the cool glass of the bedroom window. When I finish, I will push my feet into running shoes and head outside to fill my lungs with salty ocean air.

In this early hour, every movement I make echoes through the rooms of the house. A home shouldn't sound so empty. But this place is far too big for one person, and I rattle around in it. The front door slams loudly behind me and I say a silent thanks that my neighbours aren't around much.

A few minutes in a slow jog brings me to the edge of the ocean. A zigzagged staircase weaves to the sand at the bottom of the cliffs. My body is warm, it's aching for the workout. I lengthen my stride and follow the narrow strip of beach between granite cliffs and water.

Something ahead of me grabs my attention. At first, I think it's a large lump of seaweed, but I'm wrong.

It's a woman. She's fully dressed, and I think immediately that it's suicide. She wasn't spat up by the sea but dropped from the cliffs above.

Is there a chance she's not dead? I push into a sprint to reach her. Maybe she's drunk, or has broken her ankle, or just likes to sleep face-down on the beach, dressed for work.

Black pants, black jacket. One low-heeled shoe on her left foot; her right foot bare. Her hair is wet and there are strings of kelp draped across her back.

Before I turn her over there's a small twinge of hesitation in my mind. Every crime show I've ever watched has taught me that it's wrong to move the body. There's a small part of me that believes she could be alive. I drop down, my knees digging into the hard sand beside her. It's been years since I've been to church but I give a silent prayer that she might be okay. With both hands, I roll her over.

The sand falls away from her in clumps. There's no colour in her face. Her skin is an opalescent white, with shades of blue and purple thatched around her eyes and lips. I don't find a pulse when I put my fingers to her throat.

She can't be much older than thirty. We'd be the same age, plus or minus a few years. Her hair is red like my own, but a darker hue. She's slim, she could be a runner like me.

As I move away, I notice the deep red marks that circle her neck. Something was wrapped around and pulled tight. This wasn't a suicide.

It takes a minute for the shock to pass, but I call 000.

'I found a dead body,' The words tumble out of my mouth, unsteady.

'Can you give me your location?' says the operator.

I describe the car park at the peak of the Cliff Road. From there they will see the staircase to the beach. If they can find the staircase, they'll find me.

'Okay. You're doing a good job. I need you to stay calm for me. Can you check if the person is breathing?'

'She's dead.' Of course she's not breathing.

I drop the phone. Stepping backwards, I keep my eyes on the woman. I don't know why, no more harm can come to her. A sharp edge juts into my back. My body is firm against the cliff face. All I can do is wait.

Small waves crash behind me, the tide creeping inwards.

Seagulls squawk in the distance.

If I strain, I can hear a distant siren that I hope is the police. The sound disappears and I'm left with only the waves crashing.

The water is creeping in. If they don't come soon, I'll have to leave her here at the mercy of the tide. Or bring her up the steps myself. Finally, I hear rushed footsteps on the worn wooden staircase. Two paramedics with a stretcher and two police officers descend on the beach.

'What's your name?' It's a man asking me, a police officer. He's turning me away from the woman and pushing me towards the old staircase. I glance over my shoulder; I feel like I shouldn't leave her like that.

'Isobel Franco,' I answer.

He nods. 'I know your parents, I think. They used to run the take-away shop, right?'

I nod. I get that a lot. A lot of locals remember my grandfather as well, but no-one mentions him. He was less popular.

The officer takes me up the stairs to the car park. He tells me his name is Steve. His name tag agrees. There's a police car and an ambulance. A female paramedic wraps a crinkled silver blanket around my shoulders.

'Is there someone we can call?' Steve says.

His voice is deep and slow. It's kind of comforting. Are police trained to talk this way?

'No.' There's no-one I would bother this early on a Sunday morning. My mother would cause a scene. My father would worry. My friends are all in Melbourne, too far away. I just want to go home.

'Well, you don't need to stay any longer,' he tells me. 'We can get you to come into the station for a formal statement later.'

I'm left sitting on a park bench still wrapped up in foil for what seems like an eternity. As my body gets colder I wonder if I should walk. It's not that far.

I watch the two paramedics struggle up the staircase with a stretcher, the body of the woman concealed. I don't watch them load her into the back of the ambulance, but the slam of the back doors closing makes me shudder.

Eventually, Steve the police officer drives me home himself, he knows my address.

It only takes a few minutes to travel back up the Cliff Road to my house. The car lulls, he puts it in park but doesn't turn off the engine. I'm glad. I don't want him to come inside.

My grandfather built this house. It's two storeys high, with a grey stone facade that looks toward the loneliness of Bass Strait. For the last four years it's been mine, but it was only a two months ago I moved in.

'Will you be okay? There are services you can access. It's a horrible thing to find. It's hard on police and we're trained for it,' Steve asks.

'I'm okay,' I nod. I move my hand to open the door, but something stops me.

I turn back around to Steve. 'The woman. What was her name?'

'No-one told you?'

'No. I don't think so.'

'Veronica Hayes.'

I nod. It's not familiar.

'She was very young. Too young,' he says, his hands still on the steering wheel and his eyes looking through the windscreen. 'She had the same birthdate as you.'

'How do you know my birthday?' I ask.

'Same way I know your address,' he smiles. 'We looked up your driver's licence while the paramedics were with you. Standard procedure.'

I nod and slide out of the passenger seat. 'Was she local?'

He nods. 'Yep. I'm surprised you don't know her.'

Cape Cross is a small town. Everyone knows everyone. We're the same age, we should have moved in the same circles. There's only one secondary school in Cape Cross and I would remember her if she went there. Perhaps she moved here as an adult. Or I don't know as many people as I think I do.

As I unlock the front door and step inside my house, I can't help but want to know who she is and how she ended up dead on a deserted beach.

2

MAYA

It's not the police who tell me that my best friend is dead. Not my husband or her mother. It's Facebook. It's a god-damned Facebook post. It's public and right at the top of my news feed. There are already hundreds of comments underneath. The condolences tumble down the page from people whose names I never heard her speak. Did any of them love her like they claim? Could they have known anything real about her?

I'm sitting on the bed in our spare room. The chatter of my two boys floats from the front of the house. They'll be all right on their own a bit longer. I reach for my phone and unlock the screen.

David has called me; he must be reading the same Facebook post as I am. The phone vibrates in my hand, his name and picture flash on the screen. My insides clench; I don't answer. I suck in a long breath of air while I wait for it to go to voicemail. I'm smart enough to not press the red 'decline' button. It's a dead giveaway you are avoiding a call.

When it stops, I tap on Veronica's name. Holding the phone to my ear, I listen to the line ring, eventually going through to her voicemail. I try again. Same result. I put the phone down and go back to my laptop.

With shaking hands, I scroll through the comments looking for a familiar name. I need to know if this is real or a hoax. I want proof.

'Mum! Mum!' I hear his voice before the six-year-old bursts through the door. It's Noah. It's always Noah who's the first to tell. 'Jacob won't let me have the Netherworld.'

'Is it your turn?' I ask, my voice cracking.

'Yes!' He places his hands on his hips in defiance. His honey-coloured hair flops over his eyes.

'Then go tell him you can have the Lego for a while.' I would go mediate myself but I'm too shaken up. All I can do is look at my open laptop. If I look into his eyes, I will cry. If I start crying, I won't stop.

Noah retreats from the bedroom, and I listen to his footsteps pad down the hallway. I am cross-legged on the bed. This is the place I come in the house when I want five minutes alone. It doesn't always work.

The playroom is at the front of the house, but I can hear Noah reading his twin the riot act.

Veronica's face is staring back at me from Facebook. It's been less than a day since I saw her. Less than twenty-four hours. It can't be true. This is mistaken identity. Someone who looks like her is dead, not Veronica. That happens, doesn't it? Or this is a cruel joke by someone she's upset.

The post itself doesn't give the cause of death or any details, but you only have to read through the first ten comments to find it. They found her body early this morning at the base of the cliffs. People are saying she jumped. That can't be true. She would never.

The photo someone has posted is the headshot she uses for her work profile. Her long hair is secured in a French twist. There's a pair of square, dark-framed glasses on her face. She never wore her glasses, they sit in the console of her car gathering dust and scratches. It doesn't quite look like her. She's too made up; trying too hard.

But that's her game. Expensive suits, crisp shirts and glasses to make her look smarter. She gave her work so much time. Max first. Work second. And then the leftovers for the rest of us.

I keep scrolling through the comments. There's a few familiar names, but no one close to her. Not her parents. Mostly a lot of clients. The kind of people she might only see once a year. If it was family commenting, I'd know for sure.

Not that I spend any time with her family. Her mother, Heather, is not nice at all. She cut in line once at the supermarket. Another time, she honked me at the roundabout near the school when I didn't take off fast enough. Small things, but enough to make me not like her.

I shouldn't be thinking about that now. It seems petty. That woman, however beastly, is in the worst pain a human can experience.

My phone is flush against my thigh. I could call her mother. I don't have Heather's number, but it wouldn't be hard to find. In fact, Veronica's laptop is under my bed. She left it here two nights ago. I'm sure I could find the number in her contacts. That way I would know for sure. If there's one thing I know about Veronica, it's that she would never commit suicide. If it was her at the bottom of the cape cliffs, then there was a terrible accident.

There is a shout so loud at the front of the house that I sit bolt upright in shock and my hands clutch on the bedspread either side of my hips. It's Jacob. Although they are identical twins I can always tell one from the other, even when there are walls between us.

'It's not your turn!' Jacob's voice shrieks.

It's time to play referee. Gently, I close my laptop and leave it on the rumpled quilt cover beside me. I tread on soft carpet down the hallway, muted blues and greys at every turn. It's a colour scheme I thought would be a good idea when I was pregnant. I thought it was the colour of calm, but it's also the colour of depression. As I discovered not long after David and I finished renovating.

'Noah took my Lego!' Jacob is the one standing defiantly this time.

'Why don't you play with something other than Lego, Jacob?' I ask, standing in the doorway.

The big screen TV bolted to the wall blares a colourful cartoon. The rug is lost in a sea of coloured bricks. Jacob sighs. He walks over to the pair of red toy boxes against the wall and starts pulling out their contents, toy by toy.

I back out of the playroom quietly and go back to my bedroom, leaving the door open a few inches.

I can't sit here any longer reading bullshit on social media. A blue light emits from the middle of the bed. It's my phone, it's has been ringing again. That's three missed calls from David now. But he'll have to wait. I'm going to find out if this is real.

Leaning over the edge of the bed, I pull out Veronica's laptop. It's password protected, but I know what the password is. The battery icon reads 15 percent. She left her laptop here but must have kept her charger. It's a new model and my older charger doesn't fit the port.

Settling back on the bed, I cross my legs under me. With a swipe of my thumb, I unlock my phone. I don't call David. I call Heather, Veronica's mother.

Jacob and Noah have settled in to play. All I can hear now is the crush of plastic as they pull more toys out of boxes. There's the familiar siren of a toy police car that was a favourite when they were toddlers. They don't play with it anymore.

The phone rings and rings and I can't believe Heather doesn't have voicemail. Unless she's turned it off. I probably would if my daughter was dead. Finally, there's a click of her having answered, and another silent moment.

'Hello?' a male voice answers.

'Neil?' I ask. He's Veronica's stepfather. Her father's been out of the picture for years.

'Who is this?' His reply is gruff and impatient.

'It's Maya Henry.'

'Oh,' his voice softens.

'I…' Now I'm not sure what to say. I don't want to cause him any pain. 'I was trying to get in touch with Heather. I saw-'

'It seems like everyone has seen.' He interrupts.

Another moment of silence sits between us. I hear a crash and a shout from the playroom. They will have to wait.

'Is it true?' What else can I say?

Neil sighs. 'I'm sorry, love. It is true.'

The truth hits me hard and all of my breath leaves my body. It takes me a moment to be able to speak again.

'I'm so sorry, Neil. How is Heather? Is she okay?'

'Not really.' Again, he is gruff, but he sounds more tired than angry.

'What can I do?'

'Oh, nothing. Don't worry. We've got people everywhere. We'll let you know about the funeral, I guess. I mean… we don't know. It's only been a few hours since we…' He doesn't finish his sentence.

I wait. I should end the call, say goodbye. But I can't. I need to know. 'What happened to her?'

He takes a moment to answer. 'We aren't sure. She's a good girl. I don't know who… I… I'm sorry, Maya. We can't talk about it. The police have told us not to say anything.'

The police. That means there is an investigation. This wasn't an accident, someone did this to her. I thank Neil and hang up the phone. The grief that is blooming inside of me churns with the addition of nausea. If there is an investigation, it won't be long before they want to talk to me.

The phone is still in my hands. I know I should call David back, but he's the last person I want to talk to.

Looking at the bedside table, I can see the topaz ring she bought that only fit on my thumb, but I wore anyhow. There's a novel she lent me I still haven't read. That's all I have left of her.

I pick up the ring and stare into the heart of the jewel, as if the answer to my questions is inside of it. My head feels stuffy and I am on the verge of tears, but I tell myself I can't cry yet. I have dinner to cook and washing to fold.

The doctor missed that it was twins on the first ultrasound. One of them was hiding, tucked behind the other. I should have known; I was so hungry all the time. Even now, six years since they were born, I remember that hunger.

I know a newborn is hard on everyone, but those first few months were rough. Sometimes I get a flash of the same dread return to me. The early days of twins were difficult beyond description.

Then I met Veronica. I kind of knew her, or at least her face was familiar. I'd gone to catholic school and she'd gone to the state school. I'm sure our paths must have crossed when we were teenagers.

With her own baby huddled on her chest, I watched her across a crowded room in a community centre. One of the women in our mothers' group had said something stupid. I can't even remember what it was now. It involved organic vegetables. But I caught her rolling her eyes. She didn't expect anyone to notice. When her eyes met mine, I couldn't help but smile at her. She smiled back, the wordless joke bringing us together. We were friends before we even had a conversation.

That's how it started. With our newborns strapped into slings or sleeping in prams, we confessed to each other. All the secrets of life with a small child came out. That motherhood was not what we expected. That we didn't always wash the dummy when it got spat on the floor. That we longed to sleep for more than two hours. At parks, in shopping malls, it all came out. And finally, I had someone else to talk to who didn't judge me. It was Veronica who told me about post-natal depression. She came with me to that first doctor's appointment. I don't know what would have happened if she hadn't. I might have lost my mind.

Our friendship was easy at first. It's only in the last few months that things have become complicated. But now, looking back, I can see the seeds scattered everywhere. I wonder if Veronica knew how things would turn out? Perhaps she saw it coming the first time our eyes met over baby toys and cups of tea.

I might not want to cry, but I can feel the hot tears on my cheeks. I wipe them away with the back of my hand, knowing that my makeup will have left black smudges around my eyes now.

The low hum of the garage door opening interrupts my thoughts.

'Is that Dad?' Noah calls, jumping up from a new game they are both playing.

'It's not the right time!' Jacob stays sitting, the more logical of the two, not believing his Dad could come home early.

I walk down the hallway towards the front of the house. A key clicks in the lock and the front door opens. The sound serves as confirmation. Both boys run from the playroom to the entrance, slipping on the tiles in their socks. David is there, his navy work pants dusty, white silica dust dotted on his eyebrows and the ends of his eyelashes. He hasn't showered. Like my father, before he became too sick to work, David is a stonemason. We have an agreement that he has to shower before he comes home after what happened to Dad. I guess today is an exception.

His mouth is solemn and his brow is creased with concern. He knows about Veronica, but he doesn't know if I do. He's looking at me, trying to judge my expression.

'I saw it online.' I save him the stress.

He gives a grim nod and slips his boots off next to the door. The boys rush to hug him, but he holds his palm up, making a stop sign.

'Daddy's got to get these clothes off first.' Both boys take a step back. They know the rules.

David looks past us to the back of the house. He doesn't know whether to shower or talk to me. I don't want that dust near our boys, no matter what is happening.

'I'm okay. Go shower,' I direct, even though I am a long way from okay.

David walks down the hallway, heavy in his work gear. He turns back and speaks low enough the boys won't hear. 'They're saying it's murder.'

I nod. My eyes grow hot. I'm going to cry again.

'When did you see her last?' His voice grows low and urgent.

Noah has disappeared back into the playroom, but Jacob stays.

'Yesterday,' I said. 'You know it was yesterday.'

He shrugs like he doesn't, but I've got the text messages from him to prove it.

'How was she? Was she all right when you saw her?' he presses.

'She was Veronica.' She wasn't all right. Telling him that won't help.

There is only so long before the police attach Veronica to me. Everyone knows we were friends. We were always together. At the coffee shop when she took ten minutes off work. At the park with our boys. Always.

There's no avoiding it. The police will want to talk to me soon. They will want to know everything.

3

ISOBEL

It's two days since I found Veronica's body on the beach. I feel weird, kind of cold. Like I need to eat a meal or put a jacket on, but those things won't help. I'm restless, itching to do something, but I'm clueless as to what.

Veronica Hayes is all anyone is talking about. Somehow, the police have kept it under wraps that it was me who found her. That can't last for much longer. Every time I leave the house, someone brings her up. Within a day, the word is out she was't a jumper. I saw the ligature on her neck, I already knew that.

My parents don't know it was me that found her either. My mother is prone to drama, to put it mildly. She needs to hear it from me before she hears it down the local bowls club.

I knock loudly, the last time the doorbell worked I was in high school. The forest green paint on their front door is peeling. Inside, I hear the murmur of my mother's voice.

It's Dad who opens the door. He raises his thick eyebrows. 'Isobel!' He says my name like no one else, the emphasis on the last syllable. The way it was intended to sound.

Lately, I've noticed that my parents are getting old. Dad's hair has turned from salt and pepper to an ashen grey. There are age marks on the back of his hands. Every time I see Mum, there's a new ailment. A limp or a cough.

'Hi Dad.' He opens the door fully and takes a step back.

He's wearing a worn burgundy jumper that must be as old as me. His hair is tousled, like he's been wearing a hat. I wonder if he's been out on the water already this morning.

'Your mother's in the lounge. She's hurt her foot feeding the dog.'

'Again?' Last year she had a fracture and walked around in a moon boot for six weeks.

There's a strange expression on my Dad's face. Part grimace. Part guilt. You can never quite predict when she is going to hurt herself. The house is full of ramps and handrails he installed, but it's never enough.

'It's not your fault, Dad. It happens.'

He shrugs as if he doesn't believe me. 'Be nice to her, yes?' He presses his lips together, then slowly turns around, not waiting for me to answer.

He does everything slowly, my father. It's something more than patience. I guess that's why he's a fisherman. He'll wait all day for them to bite, with no sudden movement to scare them away. Or perhaps the fish taught him to be like that. I'll never know.

The entry to my parents' home is small and has mirrored tiles on the longest wall to make the room seem bigger. They're so out of fashion now, they must be due to come back in again. Nothing has changed in this house in my lifetime. Not the dark orange 1970s kitchen or the avocado green bathtub.

Before I follow him inside, I clutch his wrist so he pauses. He turns back to look at me. 'Do you need money?' I ask in a low voice.

He smiles. 'No, Isobel.'

'But for the medical bills?'

'This is why I love Medicare. It's the best thing about this country.' He gives a smile and then makes his way to his armchair.

To watch my parents struggle through retirement while I live in luxury by the sea goes against the order of how things should be. But that was how my grandfather wanted it. There was even a provision in the will that prevented me from giving them money. I did anyway. It turns out you can't will from the grave. But there was only so much of my help they will accept.

I've never learnt how to be subtle about it. God knows, I've tried. But subtle is not my style.

'We're not taking any more money, Isobel.' His voice is low and steady, in tones honeyed by his accent. If you want to know if he is angry, you have to listen closely to these tones. He has never risen his voice to me. 'You have your own future to think about.'

He was born in South America and was a student in Santiago before he left the country. After that he met my mother in Australia. I don't know when he left or why. He won't talk about it.

Mum's eyes widen with a smile when she sees me. She's sunk in a lounge chair with her foot propped on a low timber stool. Her round face is pink, her red hair in tight curls.

I eye her foot, wishing she'd take better care of herself. Two years ago, she was diagnosed with brittle bone disease. It was a late in life diagnosis and her case is mild. Still, she's prone to fractures.

'This is a nice surprise,' she says.

'Hi, Mum.'

A strange look passes between the two of them. They're glad to see me, but I've interrupted something. My parents have always kept the uglier parts of their own lives from me.

They've been through a lot. I get it. My father wears his long-sleeved cotton shirts even on the hottest days of the year. I saw the scars once when I was a kid. I know some people can't talk about their own pain. Then there is my mother, who can't hide her injuries, but never would. She has her support group lunches and her groups on social media. She couldn't keep a secret if her life depended on it.

'Sit down and your Dad will make us some tea.'

I sink into the sagging red armchair opposite hers. Dad takes his cue and goes into the kitchen.

'I'll get the kettle on then,' he says.

My mother doesn't answer. Her sharp eyes are taking me in. 'You don't seem well,' she states it as a matter of fact, not an enquiry.

I shrug. 'It's been a rough couple of days.'

She keeps her eyes on me, waiting for an explanation.

'I'll tell you. First, tell me what happened to your foot.'

My mother looks down at the heavy boot on her right foot. 'Like your Dad said. I was feeding the dog.'

'What, did you trip over him?' They had a fluffy black thing that barked a lot.

'I didn't trip over anything, I lost my footing. One moment I was upright, the next I was sprawled on the patio.' She turns her face away from me.

I hear the rush of boiling water and the chink of ceramic cups from the kitchen.

'Don't forget biscuits,' calls Mum.

'Never,' replies Dad.

'What did the doctor say?' I ask.

'Oh, not much.' Her tone is dismissive.

Dad came in, placing three cups of tea on the glass coffee table in the centre of the room. 'You know your Mum, Isobel. She has her health problems.'

'But what if it's something else?'

'Nothing else is wrong,' says Mum. 'Anyway. You were going to tell me why you look like such a mess. It's not Ben, is it?'

'No.' I don't want to hear my ex-boyfriend's name. It's only been a few months since he ended things. 'Something happened. I wanted to tell you before someone else did.'

'What happened?' Dad's voice questions as he sets a plate of biscuits down. 'Is everything all right? Are you all right?'

'I'm fine. Everything's fine.'

'What then?' asks Mum. The wrinkles on her forehead etch deeper than usual.

'I was running Sunday morning. On the beach, down by the cliffs…'

'What are you doing running down there? What if the tide came in?' interrupts Dad.

'It's fine, I know the tides. I run the beach most days.'

He lets out a disgruntled sigh.

'Anyway. There was… a body. I found it. I called the police. She was a woman around my age. Her name was Veronica Hayes.'

They exchange a glance.

'Did you know her?' I ask, surprised.

Dad shakes his head. 'No. But I know who she is. I've seen her ads.'

'We heard that her body was found yesterday morning,' says Mum. 'Very sad. I know her mother, Heather.'

'What ads?' I ask.

'She's a real estate agent,' says Mum. 'She's on that billboard at the netball club. She's got a little boy, he's six.'

How was it they both knew all these things about her and I had never heard her name?

'What happened to her? How did she die?' asks Dad.

'It's an open investigation. I might be questioned again.'

'Questioned? Why would you need to be questioned? If you let them question you it makes you a suspect, Isobel!' Mum says, straightening her back and sitting upright.

'It doesn't make me a suspect.'

'You should have just stayed away. Let someone else find her. Now you're involved,' she huffs.

'You think you need a lawyer?' Dad asks.

'No! God, this conversation got out of hand quick. I just wanted to tell you it was me that found the body. Her. Veronica.' I stand up. 'I didn't want some nosy neighbour to tell you and worry you over nothing.'

That ship might have sailed. Both of their faces are pinched with concern. They have little faith in the police, after what happened to my father. I can tell him this is a different country than where he grew up, but he just smiles and calls me naïve.

'Have your tea,' my father points to the cup on the table.

I sigh and sit back down, although I want to leave. They're making a big deal out of a small thing. Picking up the lukewarm tea, I take a sip.

'We have the same birthdate,' I say.

'What?' asks my father.

'Veronica Hayes. She has the same birthdate as me. And she grew up around here. I didn't know her. Or, I don't remember her.'

Mum turns to me, she opens her mouth to speak, but Dad interrupts her.

'It's a horrible thing to discover, sweetheart. Do you want to stay here for a few nights?' he asks.

My Mum's head shoots up, staring daggers into him. But, it's her house and I don't want to be here anyway.

'No, it's okay. I'm going to her funeral on Friday,' I say.

They both look surprised. Dad stands up and places an arm on my shoulder. 'Is that a good idea? It might not be what her family wants.'

'That's true.' The idea has only just occurred to me.

Mum sighs. 'You should stay away. Like you said, you didn't know her.'

I look over at her. Not getting involved in something isn't part of her ideology.

'Sometimes it's better to leave things be,' she says quietly.

4

MAYA

Every Tuesday is shopping day. Not shopping for me, but for my father. I might be grieving but he still needs to eat. He's long past being able to drive or even walk around a super-market on his own. His oxygen tank is now a permanent attachment.

His laboured breathing is so loud I hear it over the car radio. In and out, a slow wheeze that rattles as he exhales. I hate the sound, it's a terrible reminder that his lungs have an expiry date that is fast approaching.

'I'm sorry about your friend,' he says.

I nod.

'Have you spoken to Heather?' he asks. I think he played cricket with Veronica's stepfather when they were younger.

'Only Neil, on the day they found her. They sounded over-whelmed.'

'They would be,' he says with a huff. 'What an awful thing.'

I turn into the supermarket car park.

'Nasty business,' he adds. I hope it's the end of the conversation. It hurts to talk about her.

'You got a list today?' I ask as I pull into the closet park to the supermarket entrance.

'Yep.'

I like to do Dad's shop first thing in the morning. I can get a spot right next to the front door and we have the empty supermarket to ourselves. It would be easier if he gave me the list and I came here alone. Better still I could do the whole lot online. He won't have it though. He won't let go of anything he can still do for himself, no matter how small.

He might be a slow mover, but he doesn't waste time. He pulls his oxygen tank with his right hand, reaching for canned beans and packets of biscuits with his left. The wheels of the trolley squeak underneath me as I follow him up and down the aisles.

'You seen this stuff?' He holds up a packet of microwave rice before dropping it in the trolley.

'Yeah,' I smile. He can cook a meal as long as he doesn't need to stand up too long. Using the oven is hard, but the microwave is a godsend.

When we reach the checkout, Dad pulls his wallet from his back pocket. I lay a gentle hand over his. 'I've got this one.'

He gives a humble nod and slides his wallet back into his pocket. I know he feels embarrassed, but he shouldn't. It's not Dad's fault things have gone this way. His work poisoned him and his insurance company cheated him.

'You're a good girl, Maya,' he mumbles. 'Always were.'

The only time he ever took off work was when Mum got sick. Even then, he would go back to work for weeks at a time in between her chemotherapy appointments. It was only five years after that he got sick himself. It started with coughing and wheezing. He had no history of smoking and wasn't asthmatic. The diagnosis was dropped on us quickly.

It was always terminal; the question wasn't if, but when. And then it came down to logistics. Could he stay living in his home or would he need care? Should he come and live with us?

None of us thought about money, not at first. That's what insurance is for. There was a two hundred thousand dollar payout in his policy in the case of permanent disability. This included terminal illness. They didn't deny the claim. Instead, they paid out the amount in segments. Twenty thousand dollars each year for ten years.

That doesn't sound so bad, right? Except he had no income and the twenty grand barely covered his medical expenses. Let alone his mortgage or groceries. David and I have a big mortgage hanging over our heads, but we've made it work.

Dad has used his payout to pay his own mortgage while David and I cover everything else.

The option of me going back to work was never there. Between running the boys around and helping Dad, there is no time for it. Plus, there aren't a lot of job opportunities in Cape Cross. A lot of work is seasonal, based on the tourist trade in the warmer months. We were lucky that David has his job as a stonemason. Like my Dad used to be. That's how we met.

David's job is a massive threat to his health, but he can't quit. There's no other way he'd make the same money. Without that money, my Dad is up the creek without a paddle. David can't quit while my father is alive. It's a grim thought, but it's true.

Once Dad dies, we will get the rest of his insurance policy and we can sell his house. With no siblings, the money will come straight to me. We can pay our Goliath of a mortgage right down and refinance. David can work wherever he wants. I could get back into design work.

Between now and then, I hope that poison dust stays out of David's lungs. If only so my sons have a father. And, while it's awful, I know he'll keep working there and putting himself at risk.

'When the hell did bananas get so expensive?' Dad mutters to himself as we walk back to the car. He holds the receipt in his hand.

'There was a storm up north. Ruined the season.'

He shakes his head, folding up the receipt with his free hand and stuffing it into his back pocket. He leans against the car while I load the grocery bags into the boot. Once everything is in the car, I open the passenger door and help him inside. This trip leaves him more tired each week.

'You know, I've got to ask David a favour. Is he around on the weekend?'

I answer as I turn the engine and push the car into reverse. 'Yeah, he should be. What do you need?'

He takes a deep breath. 'I want to sell some of my tools. I was going to get him to take a look. See if he can help me.'

'What are you doing that for?'

'Well, I'm in no shape to use them, am I?' He lets out a quiet laugh.

I smile. 'I'm sure he can if that's what you want.'

He nods and turns his head to look out the window.

'Wait…' I say. 'Do you need money for something?'

Dad doesn't answer straight away. 'The nurse was around last week. She says I need to change some things. Add handrails around the place. I'll need a modified bed. But by the sounds of things, it's a pricey thing to do.'

'Dad, you should have told me. David can take care of the handrails. And as for the bed, we can pay for it.'

He shakes his head. 'You've done enough, Maya. You've got two boys to think about.'

I press my lips together and take a long inhale. That rusting pile of tools would be lucky to get a hundred bucks. His car was sold months ago. The furniture in the house is as old as me. Dad's not getting that bed unless David and I pay for it.

'David will come and do the handrails on Saturday. Do you know where you want them?'

'More or less,' he nods.

'I'll get him to call you tonight. He can figure out the details with you.' He won't want to do it, he'll want to go surfing. Like he does most weekends. But I will push against the delicate balance that sits between us and force him to help my Dad.

'And the bed, what kind of bed are you thinking about?'

He speaks in a low voice. 'A hospital bed. It'll mean we can adjust it. It might help with my lungs if I can sleep with my chest elevated. Also, if I need a wheelchair, I'll be able to get in and out on my own.'

'Dad, if we get to that point, you need to move in with us.'

'I'm not doing that, Maya. You've got your own family.'

'It's not-'

He interrupts me. 'That's not up for discussion. There's another thing. Something I have to ask you for.'

'What?' I glance across at him. He's not a person who asks for anything.

'I don't want to go into a hospice.' He's wincing as he speaks the words.

'Of course not. No one wants you to,' I say. It's as close as he has come to anything but stoicism towards his condition. 'You don't need that. You're doing fine.'

'No. Not like that. I want to die in my home. It was terrible for your mother.'

The memory hits me like a slap. The small, white hospital room. The strange smell of baby powder and iodine mixed with something sweet. My mother's pale face, her eyes always closed, death hanging over her like a cloud.

'No, I don't blame you.'

'The nurse says it's possible. But I'll need some things. The bed's one of them.'

I nod. 'We'll work it out, Dad.'

'So, ask David, will you? He might know someone who wants some new tools.'

I take him home and put the groceries away. His house is clean. Things still seem in order.

Later on, I go home. A quick online search brings me to a website for home medical supplies. Dad is right, it is expensive. It doesn't take long to find the right handrails; I add six to the shopping cart. There's hospital beds too. The simplest one runs into the thousands of dollars. It goes into the cart as well.

With fast fingers, I enter Dad's address for delivery. Just as quickly, I put in my credit card details. This will take us close to the limit. But what else am I supposed to do?

5

ISOBEL

I was betting on a big turnout, and I wasn't wrong. The church car park is overflowing and I'm forced to park my car two streets away. I join the stream of mourners walking towards the service for Veronica.

It's cool for a morning in October. It rained overnight, and the air is still heavy with moisture. The sky is clear and pale above me.

The crowd is reassuring. I'll be able to slip in and stay up the back. The plan is no one will notice that I've turned up to a funeral of someone I never met.

I haven't slept well since that Saturday morning I found Veronica on the beach. I've been Googling her, looking at photos. Wondering what her life was like and how it ended too soon. It's been eating away at me. I'm hoping that today will help.

My understanding of her is limited by social media, the image she projects into the world is one of her choosing. It might not be the true Veronica. Or all of Veronica. She sold houses for a living. She had dark red hair and was attractive. There's no trace of a boyfriend I can find, but there are plenty of pictures of her son. She had a lot of friends on Facebook, but that doesn't mean she did in real life.

The police officer at the scene gave me a number for a counsellor. A soft-spoken man picked up and spoke to me for thirty minutes. He thought going to the funeral was a good idea, and that nothing about what I felt was unusual.

As I get close to the church, I spot a familiar figure.

It's been years since I've seen Maya, but I recognise her from the opposite side of the carpark. Her pale blonde hair stands like a bright flame against the dark stone wall.

We went to the catholic secondary school together. Good enough friends that I still have her number. Not close enough that I've seen her more than five times in the last decade. I'm no good at friendship.

Instead of walking to the door to the church, I head around the side to where she is standing.

'Maya!' I call to get her attention.

Maya looks up, a weak smile appears on her face as she recognises me. As I get closer, I notice the dark patches under her eyes. Her make up is already smudged. I should have left her alone.

'Isobel? Hey!' As I reach her, she wraps one arm around my neck in a half hug, the other holding a cigarette. 'I heard you were back in town.'

I nodded. 'Since when do you smoke?'

'I don't.' She frowns and looks down at her hand. 'It's a stress thing.'

Maya flicks the cigarette to the wet grass beneath us and stomps it out with a black boot.

'I didn't realise you knew Veronica,' she says. 'I'm so sorry.'

'Were you friends?' I ask.

She nods, her face falls and her pale lips press into a straight line. 'Yeah, we were good friends.' She looks towards the entry to the church. People have stopped going inside and are standing out the front. It must be full. 'This doesn't feel real.'

'I didn't know her,' I say.

'No?'

I shake my head.

'Why did you come? Do you know Heather and Neil?'

'I was running on the beach last weekend. I was the one who found her.'

'Oh,' The words leave her mouth and she looks even sadder than she did before. 'That's awful.'

There's a long silence between us. I shouldn't have come here.

'Was it...' Maya pauses. 'What did it look like? Do you think it would have been bad for her? Painful?'

'It's hard to say. I wasn't sure she was dead.' I can only tell her the truth.

Maya nods. I don't know if I've said the right thing.

'We should go inside. I want to stay up the back. Will you sit with me?' she asks.

'Of course,' I answer.

Someone catches my eye as Maya and I walk through the entrance to the church. Tall and well dressed in a navy suit, with a crop of neat silver hair. I know him, but I can't place him. As I pass, he doesn't blink. It's like he wants to stare me down.

'You know him?' asks Maya in a low voice once we've passed.

'I can't place him but he looks familiar.'

We slip into the back of the church. It takes a minute, but it hits me.

'Edmund Keane,' I whisper out loud.

'Huh?' asks Maya.

'That guy who was staring. He's a solicitor.'

'Oh.' Maya sounds confused.

'He probably thinks I'm here to compete for business with him.'

She nods, but her eyes focus ahead. Edmund Keane had been around forever and was the only other lawyer in this town. Not that I had been working the last two months since I came back to Cape Cross. I'm not sure why he is threatened by someone like me. Anyhow, my drive to start my practice was diminishing every day.

I ignore him, moving my gaze towards the front of the church. It's a small, old building. The floorboards are original and the pews are scratched but sturdy.

The cherry-coloured coffin is topped with a cascade of white flowers. Ahead of me is a sea of black and grey. There is a mumble of conversation, people keep their voices low.

Someone catches my eye. I can only see his outline from behind, but I'd recognise him anywhere. No one would forget the broad shoulders and the slight curl to his sandy coloured hair. How long has it been since I've him? It must be years.

I need to take a leaf out of my mother's book and learn how to stalk a person on social media. Like me, he split for Melbourne after high school. I didn't realise he'd come home.

'Poor Liam,' says Maya. She has followed the direction of my eyes.

'Poor Liam?' I repeat his name.

She looks over, regarding my expression. She knows he's my ex. 'They were together a few years back. Liam and Veronica. Sorry, I thought you would have known.'

'Oh.' My stomach sinks and I'm reminded of why I don't stalk my exes on social media. I'd rather not find out.

We stay at the back, like we both intended, leaning against the cold stone wall. The service is fast. Only Veronica's stepfather speaks, other than the celebrant. There's a projector screen, cycling through a series of photos of her life. A newborn baby. A rosy-cheeked toddler. A teenager dressed in black. It's over within thirty minutes.

The family follows out the coffin. The pallbearers first, and then a woman whom I guess is Veronica's mother. In her late fifties, she has dark hair and a short stature, collapsed even smaller by her grief. She has a relative either side with their arms around her, who are practically carrying her.

They're about to pass us, but she stops and looks up. She looks at me and her eyes fill up with horror. What could I have done wrong? She looks like she's seen a ghost. Then I realise why.

I look like her dead daughter.

6

ISOBEL

My phone is flashing, lighting up the inside of my handbag. I don't notice it while I'm outside in the daylight, but as soon as I'm in my car it catches my eye. I reach in, feeling for its smooth plastic cover, then flip it in my hand. Before I unlock it, I can tell something is wrong. The screen is lit up with messages and missed calls. They're all from my mother.

Pls call when you get this.

Isobel call me back.

Why aren't you answering? Where are you?

They have arrested your father. Please call.

Arrested? What for? He doesn't even exceed catch limits when he's out fishing. I call her back.

'What the hell, Mum?' I blurt as soon as she answers.

'I don't know. I don't know. They turned up here, six of them.' Her voice is high pitched and she's talking too fast.

'They can't just take a person, Mum. They have to tell you what the arrest is for.'

'I don't know,' she repeats herself. She sounds angry now, like she's annoyed at me for not understanding.

I'm still sitting out the front of the church, in the driver's seat of my car. Funeral mourners are dispersing, filing away to their own cars and homes. Their sombre mood doesn't match the frequency of the phone conversation I'm having.

'Okay. Take a breath.'

She doesn't respond, and I can only hope she's taking my advice.

'Exactly what happened?'

'There were six police officers,' she says.

'Uniformed police?' I asked.

'Yes.'

'Did you get any of their names?'

'There wasn't any time for that.'

'And what did they say? Word for word, as close as you can remember.' Six cops don't show up for a fishing violation. I can't imagine what else my father could be tangled up in.

'That they wanted to question him. That he needed to go to

the station.' Well, that's different than being arrested. It could be anything. It could be a tax matter from five years ago. It could be unpaid parking tickets.

'Can you remember if they gave him a caution?' I ask.

My mother hesitates. 'A caution?'

'Reading him his rights, like on television.'

She is silent for a moment, as if remembering. 'I don't think so. Should I have gone with him?' No. My mother has a flare for the dramatic. Her going along would be a terrible idea. Plus, I doubt the police would have allowed it.

'Where did they take him?'

'I don't know. The station here, I guess. What do I do, Isobel? Imagine what he's thinking right now. You know what happened to him.'

Actually, I don't know because he never speaks about it. I can only guess. It must have been awful. But he comes from a time when men didn't talk about feelings.

'I'm going down to the station, Mum. I'm not far away. Just sit tight, okay? And try not to worry.'

There's a pause between us and I think she's hung up. But then she speaks.

'He will need a lawyer,' she says, her voice quiet.

'Mum?' I question her. 'What does he need a lawyer for? What aren't you telling me?'

'What if it's about Veronica Hayes?' she says.

I sigh and lean back into the upholstery of my car. Here we go with the drama again. 'It's not, Mum.'

'What if it is? What if because you found her…'

'Mum! Calm down. Maybe he forgot to pay a parking fine.'

She tried to speak again, but I cut her off. 'I'm going to go down the station. Look, I'll call you when I find out more.'

It crosses my mind to pick her up and take her in with me. There's little chance she can drive with her foot in a boot. The thought of her conspiracy theories in the car and at the police station are too much, so I go alone.

The police station is less than a kilometre away, but it's slow moving. There's a bulge of traffic leaving the funeral and slow-walking pedestrians everywhere. As I drive, I rack my brain again for an explanation.

It's a mistake. My dad is a good guy. He's quiet. He was around when I was a kid. He did everything a dad is supposed to do. It's hard to fault him.

It could be something to do with the shop, although it's been years since they sold it. Could it be linked to Veronica Hayes? When I dropped in the other morning, there was something odd about the way my parents acted. It could be anything though. Maybe they were having a fight.

I park out the front of the police station. This part of town is quiet and there are no other cars or people around. The building is new, square and rendered in a dark grey. It's modern for a small town, the old weatherboard station being replaced a few years back.

When I get inside, it's even quieter. There's a small reception area, with a linoleum floor, no chairs and a hard Perspex screen between me and whoever is sitting behind the desk. The only point of entry to the rest of the station is through a heavy door with a pin code on in.

A female officer sits on the other side of the desk, her blond head pointed downwards at a pile of paperwork. After a few beats, she looks up.

'I'm looking for my Dad,' I say. She blinks, peering at me a moment longer than feels comfortable.

She nods as if nothing is wrong. 'Mr Franco will be out soon.'

'Is he under arrest?'

Her smile flatlined. 'Unless you're his lawyer, I can't tell you that.'

She's tougher than she looks.

'Does he need a lawyer? Has he been cautioned?' My voice is as flat as her expression.

The edges of her mouth creep upwards again. 'He'll be along shortly.'

I should sit down, but there's nowhere to sit. She wants me to leave, but I wait in the cold reception area for the chance I overhear something. For now, there's only the hum of a computer and the occasional scratch of the officer's pen on paper. More than likely, the walls are soundproofed.

It's close to half an hour of waiting in the small room. Finally, the door makes a loud clicking sound as it's unlocked from the other side. It opens, and my father walks through. A uniformed police officer stands in the doorway, watching him leave.

My father's eyes meet mine. His expression is glassy, the lines on his face are more pronounced. I don't want to be the first to talk, so instead I motion to the exit door.

I can feel the eyes of both police officers on us as we walk to the street. With a click on the remote, I unlock my car. My father opens the passenger door and sits inside. Once my door is shut, I wait for him to speak. It feels like an eternity is passing.

'I'm so sorry, Isobel,' he finally says.

7

MAYA

I am living one problem at a time. One day at a time. No, scratch that. An hour at a time. My movements are methodical; I remind myself how to get out of bed or how to walk into a kitchen. It's like the basic instructions of life which were once inscribed into my brain have been obscured by a thick, dark fog.

Six days have passed, and each has shown me a new type of pain. Each morning, I shower and dress. I put food in my mouth, chew it and swallow. David has been watching me, asking after me. It feels like he's always a step or two behind me, a shadow in the house.

David stayed home with Jacob and Noah while I went to Veronica's funeral. There wasn't any other option. Dad is too sick to watch them on his own now. David's family are in Melbourne. Everyone else we know would be in attendance. So I ended up going to my best friend's funeral alone.

The police released Veronica's body to her family. They've made no statement. It might have been a suicide spot, but the town is full of murder talk. If they are investigating anything, they are doing it quietly. Maybe they're not coming for me.

This morning was the funeral. The arches of my feet are on fire and all I can think about is getting these silly boots off. I park my car in the garage, next to David's ute.

Once I'm inside, I pull off my boots and leave them at the front door. I hear laughter in the playroom. They've brought in all the chairs from the dining room and hung blankets across them, making a giant fort.

'How was it?' David asks, sticking his head through two suspended blankets.

'Sad,' I reply. 'It's real now. I've spent the last week going to pick up the phone to call her… and then I remember.'

He says nothing. The boys must have cars in their fort, they're making engine noises. The soles of their feet stick out from one side. Those four feet seem so small and clean and innocent. The last few months have been so hard.

'I might go take a shower.' I lean my neck to one side and hear a crack.

'Okay,' he says. 'Any talk on what happened?'

I shake my head. Maybe the truth won't ever come out. As I turn towards the master bedroom, I hear a knock on the front door. Through the cloudy pane of glass, I can make out a pair of shadowy figures.

'I'll get it,' I say.

'Okay,' David replies, getting pulled back into the blanket fort by the twins.

I'm tired. I want this day to be over.

I open the door to find two sombre looking police officers in their dark navy uniforms.

'Maya Henry?' Asks the one on the left, a woman a few years younger than me. Her tied-back hair is shining onyx and her eyes emerald. She's wearing no make-up, but she would look beautiful if she did.

I nod. 'Yes.'

'I'm Senior Sargent Stacey Collins. This is Senior Constable Dax Martin.' She gives a sideways nod of her head to her colleague beside her. He is younger again, hanging a step behind.

'Okay.'

They both wait. She holds eye contact with me. Do they want me to ask them in?

'Is everything all right?' I say.

She nods. 'We'd like to talk to you about Veronica Hayes.'

'I just got back from her funeral.' My tone is curt, but I didn't care.

David has left the playroom; I can see his profile from the corner of my eye.

'Can we come in?' The other officer comes forward as he speaks.

'Okay,' I agree. I open the door all the way. David takes a step closer and wraps an arm around my waist, protectively.

'Do you think today is really the day for this?' he asks. 'Her friend has just been buried.'

The two cops exchange a glance but don't offer any apology.

I catch David's eye. 'It's okay,' I say.

They come inside and they don't offer to take their shoes off. This is a shoes-off house. If the spotless carpets don't give that away, then the neat line of shoes against the wall should. I grit my teeth, but I say nothing.

I step into the hall and they follow. I see Stacey Collins look through the open double doors to the playroom. Its mess of Lego, toy cars and blanket fort are in full view.

'There's another room we can sit in at the back of the house,' I say. They both give small nods of their heads in acknowledgement. I turn to David. 'Can you keep the boys busy?'

'I think I should be in there,' he replies.

'It's fine.' I shake my head.

'You don't have to talk to them at all if you don't want to. Especially not today,' he says in a low whisper.

'It's better to get it over with.'

He looks like he won't let me go, but I shrug him off and turn towards the lounge room at the rear of the house. The two officers are only a few steps behind me, and I know that they can hear everything we say. I can feel their eyes on my house, making assumptions.

I motion for them to sit on the pale blue couch in the lounge room. I take the navy armchair opposite. In the middle of the room is a chocolate-coloured coffee table, with three ceramic apples in its centre. I had to order them online and they took weeks to arrive. The boys aren't allowed in here.

'So, what do you want to talk about?' I ask.

The female cop leans forward. 'Veronica Hayes's death wasn't a suicide.'

Four eyes watch me, unblinking. The familiar tune of a kids' cartoon floats down the hallway. Thank God. David won't hear any of this. I'm half expecting him to follow me down here.

'You don't seem surprised,' says the male cop. I've forgotten his name, so I look for his name tag. Dax. What kind of name is that?

'She's not that kind of person.' After the words come out, I realise I'm talking in the present tense, like she's still here. 'She would never leave Max without a mother.'

'So, you were close.' She's making a statement, not asking a question.

'You wouldn't be here if you didn't know that.' They know

more than the fact that we were friends. Otherwise, they wouldn't be watching my reactions so closely.

'I'd like to tell you the cause of death,' says Stacey. 'But I will ask you to keep it confidential at this point in the investigation.'

I nod.

'Strangulation.' One word. That's all she says. My mind paints a horrible picture of Veronica, gasping for breath and clutching at her neck. I don't want to cry in front of these two, but I feel tears behind my eyes.

'Who do you think would do something like that to her?' she probes.

'No one.' My voice is cracking.

'What about work?' asks Dax. 'An angry client? Anyone who disliked her?'

'No one. She would have told me.' She might have upset a few people over the years. Her determination impeded her conduct. She'd mentioned a few, but never their names.

'You were with Isobel Franco this morning,' says Stacey.

'Yes.'

'Is she a friend, too?' she asks.

'We went to high school together.'

'And did she know Veronica Hayes?'

'No. Veronica went to the state school. Isobel has been in Melbourne a long time.'

They exchange another glance between themselves.

'When did you see Veronica last?' asks Dax.

I wait before I tell them, like I am thinking about it. 'Saturday morning. We met at the park.'

'Which park? And at what time?' presses Stacey.

'The big one on the foreshore, and I don't know. Maybe ten.'

'How would you describe her state of mind?'

The three boys had zipped back and forth on the flying fox, out of earshot. We had sat on the steel park bench, a foot of space between us. The conversation started as awkward and had ended angry. Me saying no to Veronica for the first time. Veronica telling me to toughen up, to get my shit together. She had never said a bad word to me before that day. But I was the one who let her down.

'Normal. She was fine.'

Stacey Collins looks me dead in the eyes. She knows I'm lying.

8

ISOBEL

I can't buy him a coffee; he doesn't drink it. Nor can I offer to buy him food. He only eats what he cooks himself. There's no chance I can take him home to Mum, not yet. She'll be a mess. So, instead of my mother's noise and outbursts, I get my father's silence.

Sometimes I think my parents are like two sides of the same crazy coin. I can't decide which one of them is worse.

I've driven to the beach. Not the surf beach or where the cliffs are, but to Safety Beach; a small inlet of sand where it's possible to swim. There's no one around. I park the car, but neither of us move to get out.

My father looks straight through the windscreen rather than meet my eye. I look in the same direction, to the silver streak of water on the horizon. It's not warm enough to swim. There's not even a dog walker out there today.

He's still not talking to me. Well, he is talking, but in blunt, single-word sentences. He's not answering questions about why he was in the police station. His affect hasn't changed. He's calm, not upset at all. When I asked how he was treated in custody, he only shrugged.

The car park is elevated. I can see the water, but only a scrap of sand. 'Do you want to go to the beach?'

'No.' He's not a person who goes to the beach unless it's for fishing.

Reaching across the car, I lay my hand on his wrist. 'What's going on?'

He shakes his head again. 'It was nothing.'

'From Mum's description it didn't sound like nothing.'

He shrugs and turns slightly to face me. 'There's a car park at the top of the cliffs. The cliffs where they found the body of Veronica Hayes.'

Only minutes before I had found her, I'd run down the jagged staircase from that carpark to the beach. 'Yes.'

'There was a van there the night before. Around the time of death. A white van.'

I make the connection. 'What and they think it was you? That's ridiculous, Dad. Who doesn't have a white van? Every tradesman in Cape Cross drives one.'

He blinks and breaks eye contact. 'Someone noticed it that night. They called the police later.'

'That's still not enough. Why would they say it was yours?'

He shrugged. 'I'm not sure who reported it or what they said to the police. Only that there is a witness. They asked me for an alibi.'

'I'm guessing you were at home.'

'Of course.'

I shake my head. The cops are grasping at straws. A surge of frustration runs through me.

'They've got nothing. They've got nothing on who killed her, so they're bringing in anyone. Trust me, Dad. I've dealt with the cops at work before. I'm the connection here. All they've got is me and a white van.' I tap my fingers on the leather steering wheel.

The police would be under pressure to make an arrest. A murder in a country town always makes an impact. Not to mention, it's only weeks from the start of the holiday season. Most of the people in this town make the bulk of their income in December and January. None of them want a murder coming up in the search results of the town's name.

Dad considers this before he speaks. 'Once I had a close friend. She was bright, and after school she studied at the university. We had no free university like here.'

It's not free. But now wasn't the time to make a point. To my father, an interest-free student loan was close enough. He gave me a sharp look, so I could tell he wasn't finished talking.

'Her doctorate was on justice. On whether justice exists.'

'Justice exists. We have a whole court system for that.'

'But who decides on what justice is? If someone breaks into my home and I shoot them, do I go to jail?'

'Probably not. Not if they were armed.'

'What if they were ill? Or they were drunk and went into the wrong house?'

'I don't know, Dad. That's why we have courts and judges.'

'Humans are the only creatures who believe in justice. Dogs don't believe in justice. Birds don't. They just live their lives, and sometimes bad and unfortunate things happen. The things I did as a young man, if I did them in Australia no one would care. No one would take any notice in Australia. But in my country, it meant prison. It meant interrogation. It meant being watched and followed. I became a rule breaker when I broke the rules they created.'

'But that wasn't right. And a whole government got overthrown.'

He paused and took a deep breath. 'Sometimes things that aren't right, but they happen. And there's nothing you can do about it.'

'What are you trying to say, Dad?'

'People go to jail for the wrong reasons all the time. They've got a van that looks like mine in a car park and my daughter finding a body. I wouldn't be the first innocent person to be sent to prison.'

How much evidence would they rely on to prosecute? It must have been the middle of the night when the witness saw them. Were they reliable? Did they remember a licence plate? And what were they even doing out on the streets?

'If you didn't do it, you didn't do it. Yon won't be prosecuted for a crime you didn't commit. They won't have the evidence, Dad.'

He shrugs again.

'Is there something you're not telling me? Another piece of evidence? What exactly did they say to you in there?'

They have him worried. It must be more than a sighting of his car.

'Let's go home,' he says. 'Your mother won't be doing well.'

He won't answer my questions.

'You didn't know her, did you?' I ask for the second time.

'Only who she was. That's all.' He's still not looking at me. He's looking straight ahead at the ocean.

9

ISOBEL

The last few nights, I've seen Veronica. Not literally. When I'm trying to fall asleep at night, a picture flashes in my mind; an image of the dark ocean lapping against pale flesh. I wake up feeling a mix of guilt and nausea.

She's dead, and I'm alive, combing through her Instagram feed. Not to learn more about her or celebrate her life either. That might be how I started, but now I'm looking for a suspect. A nasty ex-boyfriend? The only lover I know about is Liam, and he's not the jealous type.

The likelihood of me figuring it out in my study on a windy Friday night is low. There could be many reasons that she's dead. Did she wrong a lover? Or a business partner? Or did she go down the wrong path at the wrong time?

I've spent most of the last week thinking about her. Not only thinking. If she were alive, it would be considered stalking.

Before the funeral, I'd already scoured her social media pages. I go deeper. From a Google search, I find articles in the local paper. They're all related to her work.

She's attractive. Her hair is always in a neat bun and she dresses well in dark-coloured suits and crisp shirts. There's no telling what she wore on the weekend. Her social media pages give little away about her personal life.

The only exception is her son. There's a crazy amount of pictures of him. It's like going back in time. I see him as a newborn, as a toddler learning to walk. At the beginning of this year there's a picture of him on his first day of school.

There was no sign of him at the funeral. Did someone keep him away? What a terrible thing for a kid to go through. Who will be there for him now? Where is his father? I feel a heavy kind of pain in my body when I think of him. The thought of any child suffering is too much for me.

I did get pregnant, once. When I didn't conceive right away, we found a specialist, and I started hormone treatments. When that didn't work, I moved on to IVF. It was brutal, both the injections and the pain of collections and transfers. Then there was the waiting. Waiting to find out how many eggs, how many embryos. Waiting to find out if they made it to day three or day five, then if it was sticky enough to stay. From the beginning, I was aware there was only so much I could take.

Ben became distant. He left the room each time I injected myself in the stomach, morning and night. He only came to the initial appointments, never to the scans or the collections.

He felt we were failing by needing a fertility clinic at all. Later, he would claim it was me who blocked him out.

But then a transfer stuck, and everything was all right. For a little while.

If I'd didn't lose that pregnancy, I'd have a toddler of my own by now. It was an early miscarriage. I never found out if it was a boy or girl. Someone told me at the time that it's not so bad when you lose them early. It's less grief. I think that's bullshit.

After the third round of IVF, I could tell it was fruitless. My single pregnancy was almost close to impossible, statistically. My heart agreed with my brain, I would never experience another. So I quit. And eventually, Ben quit our whole relationship.

Ben was supposed to move to Cape Cross with me. We were going to fill the house I had inherited with a family. That never happened. For a time, I was lost in the hazy unhappiness of the break up, and somewhere in there I quit my job. I decided to move into the house anyway.

I have a routine. My coffee and my morning run. I try to spend the rest of the time deciding what my life should look like, now I know I can't have a family. I have no idea. I can't picture my own future anymore.

When I'm not thinking about Veronica, I'm worrying about my father. From what he's telling me, the police haven't bothered him again. My mother has nothing to say about it. And she always has an opinion on everything.

The reality is, I'm the best person to help them right now. I'm not a criminal lawyer, but I've got contacts. I know enough about the system to protect them. I also know that my father is right when he says innocent people go to prison sometimes.

Maya sent a text to ask if I'm all right. It should be the other way around, she's the one who lost a friend. She was always kind, even when we were at school. An open person, nice to everyone no matter who you were. Nicer than you need to be.

After I get to the eleventh page of Google results, there's nothing left. I get an article about a Valerie Hayes who plays netball in New Zealand. Then another about Vic Hayes, who is fundraising for cancer. I've reached the bottom of my research barrel.

The last small detail I scrape is that she was born in the bush nursing hospital. Cape Cross has never been big enough for its own hospital. We only have the local doctor who goes home at five pm. If you get into trouble after that, you'll have to go to the real hospital in Waringal, a forty-minute drive away.

Years ago, there was a bush nursing hospital. It was closed after a nurse misdiagnosed a septic patient. They died two hours after being sent home. They were under-funded and understaffed.

Ever since, the hospital building has sat deserted. The call from locals to reopen has never gone quiet. No one wants to travel to Waringal, especially if you are in an ambulance. But there's not enough people and not enough money.

A loud bang brings me to my senses. I turn around to see my

small filing cabinet has fallen over. The draw is unlocked and has slid open. The weight has toppled the whole thing. It was a cheap cabinet I picked up at an office supply store for under a hundred dollars. Serves me right that it's broken already.

Getting out of my seat, I tip the cabinet upright and slide the draw back in. Thankfully, none of the paperwork had fallen out. There's no clicking sound, so I fetch the key from my bedroom and come back and lock it. It must be faulty. There's nothing interesting in there. Mostly tax documents I need to keep for five years and some x-rays from when I sprained my ankle last year. Things that I can't scan and put in Dropbox.

I've been on my computer for hours and I could use a break. I head towards my bedroom, stretching my arms out behind me as I walk.

I'm looking out the front window into the darkness when my phone rings. God, I hate the sound of a ringing phone. After years of it ringing at me all day at work, I've started leaving it on silent. Not today, though.

With a sigh, I walk towards the back of the house where the phone rests on the kitchen bench. Private number. I don't answer. It's late, even for telemarketers.

Back at my laptop, the long list of Google search results is still up. It's frustrating. I can't sit around and see my Dad accused of something he didn't do. Just a rumour is enough to ruin you in this town. It's as good as the decision of a jury.

What other avenue did I have to explore? Even though I never met Veronica, there are a crazy amount of connections between us. We know the same people. We have friends in common, like Maya. We even have an ex-boyfriend in common in Liam. In a lot of ways, we have led parallel lives. It feels like wherever I turn, I find another link between us.

Part of me thinks I should let it go. Another part urges me on, it's telling me to push further. There's something else to find. I need to follow those links between us.

Liam Goddard is as good a place to start as any.

10

ISOBEL

The best way to punctuate a bad day is with a glass of wine, but that's not the reason I am at the pub. I've heard that Liam works here. It's a leap for someone that was a medical researcher not so long ago, but he probably has his reasons.

It's Saturday night, and it's busy, but I want to ask him about Veronica. After Maya, he's my next best connection to her. I can get a better picture of who might have wanted to hurt her.

There's two pubs in Cape Cross. The bottom pub is named because it's at the low end of Main Street. It's family friendly, they serve decent counter meals. A short drive away, up on the cliffs in a quieter area is the top pub. They don't serve anything more complicated than potato chips, but there's always cold beer. It's sticky and grungy, but the tourists stay away.

It's an old pub, two storeys tall and painted white, with the year it was built in brass letters above the front door. If you can get a table at the back, you can watch the surf roll in.

I stop at the far end of the car park, an old habit after finding my car scratched one too many times. It's dark, and there's nothing to see, but I can hear the crash of waves far below.

A white four-wheel-drive pulls into the car park as I hit lock on my remote. There's empty spots closer, but it stops right next to my car. I can't see through the dark-tinted windows. Whoever it is leaves the engine on.

When I walk in, the bright warm room is a stark contrast to the cool and quiet outside. Like I predicted, the place is busy and alive with a hum of chatter. There's no table service, so there's a solid crowd of people around the bar waiting for a drink.

'You're not a beer girl, if memory serves me correctly.' A strong, low voice speaks to me from behind. Looking over my shoulder, I see Liam Goddard. His chest is almost touching my shoulder.

'Hi,' I say. I go to turn around, but he places his hand on the small of my back, pushing me towards the main bar.

'Can't be blocking an exit. Safety issue.'

'Oh. Sorry. I was just grabbing a quick drink on the way home.'

'Come up to the bar then.'

I walk towards the bar and sit down, pulling out the stool next to me for him.

If I said Liam never crossed my mind, I'd be lying. But if I dwell on it, I'd rather not feel like I did with him again. There were a lot of good times, but also some bad ones.

He was perfect for my seventeen-year-old heart. I was slightly reserved, he was inclined towards extroversion; on paper we were perfect. He was smart and a hard worker to boot.

Reality was different. Things would be fine for weeks, then he'd forget something important and not show up. Sometimes he'd disappear for days then turn up at my door at three am. Perhaps he was so tired from holding everything together that he fell apart.

In my twenties, I still thought I had the power to change people. Each time he let me down, I took it more personally.

I confronted him eventually. He took me on a holiday to Bali to make it up to me, then turned up at the airport with no money. I ended up paying for everything. We ended things not long after. I don't want a rollercoaster ride in a partner. I want stability. Or at least predictability.

I'm doing the maths in my head and it must be four or five years since I've seen him. When was the last time? It was a bar here in Cape Cross, I think it was my birthday. I'd come home to visit my parents for the weekend. We talked a while, but I saw him leave with another woman.

I wait for him to sit on the stool beside me, but he walks

straight past me. Is he brushing me off? He steps sideways, opens a hinged gate and slips behind the bar.

'You're on the clock?' I ask.

He nods.

'How long have you been working here?'

'For two years. I manage the place.'

Liam is not someone I would peg as a hospitality worker. He's got at least two degrees, and the last time I saw him he was using the cowpox virus to destroy cancer cells. Now he's pulling beers. It didn't add up.

'What do you drink these days?' he asks.

'Any kind of red wine.'

'Well, we have a few, but all of them are terrible. I can offer you a decent beer though.'

It's a beer kind of town. 'I'll stick with bad wine.'

Liam pulls two pint glasses from under the bar and starts filling them up with the beer that's on tap. He pushes one in front of me. Did he not hear me?

'I really don't drink beer.'

'I know, but I really can't serve you the wine we keep in stock. Just on principle. I've argued for better, but I've been unsuccessful so far.'

Age suited Liam. He wore himself better; he seemed calm. Up

close, I could see the lines in the corners of his eyes now. His sandy coloured hair was still a little long, his eyes always the colour of a winter ocean.

'How long have you been back in Cape Cross?' I ask him.

He picks up his glass and takes a sip. Unlike me, he had been a beer drinker back in the day and it seemed like he still was. 'Two years. I got the job here right away.'

'You never told me.'

'Izzy, you stopped returning my calls years ago. Why would I tell you I'm around? Plus, you stayed in Melbourne.'

My eyes snap up at the sounds of that name. Only Liam had ever called me Izzy and hearing it brought on a fuzzy nostalgia. It was such a different name. Isobel was sensible and accomplished. Izzy was... someone else.

I took a sip of the beer. It wasn't terrible, but it wasn't for me.

I sighed. 'Sorry.'

He shrugged. He took a sip of his own beer.

'So you're back in town?'

'Yeah,' I answer. 'I've been here for two months now.'

'In the old house?'

'I renovated it.'

He nods. 'It's a great location.'

'So, you can drink on this job?' I ask, motioning to the beer.

'No. But the owner's never around. Anyway, I'm making an exception for you.'

He smiles, and like a reflex, I smile back. It's easy to remember why I'd liked him so much. But that was teenage love, and I was only a kid. That kind of thing rarely translates well to an adult world.

I change gears. I'm here for a reason. 'I'm sorry about Veronica.'

He nods. 'Thanks. I saw you there. At the funeral.'

'I never met her.'

'You found her though,' he says.

It must no longer be a secret that I was the one to find the body. I let out a huff of air. 'Yeah.'

Liam looks downwards, taking his eyes away from me.

'It's a horrible thing to happen,' I say. 'I know you... were friends.'

Liam's eyes flick up and meet mine. It's like he's searching for something. I'm not sure what he thinks he will find. It felt the same when Maya asked me to tell her what I saw on that beach.

I snip it in the bud. 'There's nothing I can tell you don't already know.'

He sighs, looks at the timber of the bar and taps his fingers a few times. 'I was thinking about her a lot. I Googled strangulation. That's what I heard happened. It wouldn't have been over quickly.'

'I can't even imagine.'

I wait, but he says nothing else.

'Did you see her a lot?' I tiptoe around a direct question about their relationship. Liam is grieving, like Maya had been.

'No.' He speaks quietly. 'She stopped talking to me four years ago.'

'Oh. I'm sorry.'

He nods. 'She met someone new. The word is she'd been happy of late.'

'Who?' I ask.

He shakes his head for no. 'I say we stopped talking... she ghosted me. One hundred percent. Everything I heard about her was second-hand.'

So much for Liam having answers about Veronica. Shifting on the bar stool a little, I hesitate before I ask the next question. 'Did she have enemies?'

'Enemies?' He raises his eyebrows.

'Maybe something to do with work? A deal gone bad?' If I wasn't a lawyer, I'd be wincing as I waited for his response. I'd had practise with difficult questions. A poker face was a skill worth learning.

'She was competitive at work. After she had Max, she became very driven.'

'With anyone in particular?'

He shakes his head. 'I don't think so.' He pauses for a moment. 'Did the police say something?'

'No... they only asked me basic stuff. There wasn't much I could offer them.'

His glass is empty. Mine is three quarters full.

'They called my Dad in,' I say.

'Really? What on Earth would they want your Dad for?'

'There was a van up on the cliffs around the time she was last seen. It looked like his.'

Liam narrows his eyes in disbelief. 'He'd be near the water all the time. He was probably fishing.'

'No. No fishing there. There are too many rocks. Plus, he only fishes from the boat these days. It had to be a similar vehicle. Or a bad memory.'

'They've been doing the rounds, pulling in family and friends. Between you and me, they've haven't got a clue.'

'Really?' Maybe my Dad had nothing to worry about.

'But don't repeat that, I've got a mate on the force who's working the case.'

'How did you know that I found her? The police said that they wouldn't release that information.'

He looks at me like the answer is obvious. 'It's Cape Cross. Everyone knows.'

Everyone always knows everything around here. But I have a feeling there is something I'm missing.

'We had the same birthdate. Veronica and me.'

Liam nods without skipping a beat. 'Yeah.'

'You knew that, too? God, what else are the police telling people?'

'Izzy, I know your birthday. The police didn't tell me.'

Of course Liam knows my birthday. Just like he would know Veronica's. 'You don't think that's weird?'

He shrugs. 'It's a coincidence. A September birthdate is the most common.'

'Really?'

'Everyone is on holidays nine months earlier. Christmas, New Year's Eve…' He trails off with a smirk.

I roll my eyes.

'Seriously though, there's something else you should know about Veronica.'

'What's that?' I asked.

He leans forward over the timber bar, our faces only inches apart. 'She was asking people about you an awful lot.'

11

MAYA

I'm no fan of therapists. They ask probing questions and give nothing in return. They poke at your scars and resurrect old pain. That's not something I need. It's not my first time in this chair, I've been here before.

'Do you think getting back to your routine will help you?' asks Lucy.

Her hair is sandy blonde and she's under thirty, which is young for a therapist. Like she's compensating, she's wearing thick-framed glasses and neutral-coloured clothes.

'I have two boys. I don't have a choice. They need to eat and sleep and go to school.'

I don't need answers or epiphanies. I need to get my life back in order. Not for me, but for Jacob and Noah.

Lucy nods, her expression giving nothing away. There's no

outward judgement in here. That's something that drives me crazy. In fact, this whole scenario is driving me nuts. David suggested it, but now I'm regretting coming here at all.

'I can't change what happened. But I need to do the school run.'

'It sounds like you are still blaming yourself for Veronica's death.'

Yep, we went over that in the first session. Lucy says my feelings of guilt are exaggerating my grief. And she's insisting that I accept that I can't change what happened to Veronica. That it isn't my fault. There's a thought I can't shake; without me she might not have been there.

Lucy waits, but I don't speak.

'What about your husband?'

Is she asking if I blame David for Veronica's death? 'What about him?'

'Has he been a good support?'

'Yes,' I answer. 'He's trying to keep his hours down at work, helping a little with the boys.'

'He works a lot of overtime?'

'When he can get it,' I let out a breath I didn't know I was holding.

'So you're left to do a lot with the boys.'

'Yes. I don't mind. I haven't worked since they were born.'

I'd always planned to go back. After studying graphic design, I'd built a steady flow of work, most of it remote. While I had intended to go back before I got the chance, Dad got sick.

'It's a lot for one person.'

I nod. But she can tell that I don't agree.

'You don't think so?' Lucy asks.

'Sometimes… but it's just easier to do things on my own. David can play with the boys, but he's not good at anything practical. I can't tell you the last time he did a load of washing or packed a lunchbox.'

'So, you don't want more help from him?'

'I want more help. If I asked, it would end in a fight.' I sigh at the truth of it.

'Do you fight a lot?' She tilts her head to one side after she asks the question.

'No. But I work hard to avoid it.'

She writes something down, her pen scratching on a notepad. In the moment of silence, I hear the tick of the clock behind me.

'How often do you change your behaviour to avoid a fight?'

'I don't change my behaviour.'

'That's what you just described to me.'

I shrug. I don't have an answer because I've never thought about it that way.

She leans back in the armchair. 'What has this been like for David? Was he a friend of Veronica's as well?'

The suggestion is laughable. 'No. Not so much.'

Lucy raises her eyebrows. 'They didn't get on?'

'Not so much. But they didn't spend a lot of time together.'

'That's got to be hard, when your spouse doesn't like a close friend. Any reason?'

'There was a party three or four years ago. It was Veronica's birthday. They had a fight over something silly. Someone spilled a drink and someone else got pushed. I don't know. But they had a fight and have been on bad terms ever since.'

'Someone got pushed?' she asks. 'Who?'

'I don't remember. I'd had a few drinks, to be honest.'

'So you don't know why they stopped being friendly towards each other?'

'I don't know.' I fix my eyes on the coffee table between us.

'It must have made it hard to remain friends with Veronica.'

'No.'

Lucy is holding out the box of tissues that usually sits on the table between us. I notice the hot tears on my cheeks. I'm crying again.

'I wish that night didn't happen,' I whisper, whipping the tears away.

'Me too. But it's not your fault it did. You're not responsible.'

I could tell her the whole truth. She might change her opinion on blame and responsibility then.

'Can you imagine a time in the future where you might be easier on yourself about what happened?'

A vision of Veronica appears in my mind the last time I saw her alive. It was at her house, but it wasn't Saturday morning, like I told the police. We met again later that night. I raised my fist to knock on her door, but she pulled it open before I had the chance. She smiled.

She said she wanted her laptop back. She'd accidentally left it at my house. When I got there, I had forgotten to bring it. She said it didn't matter. It was an excuse to talk to me.

'Why didn't you just come over?' I had asked her.

'You know why. David's always there,' said Veronica, crossing her arms, standing in her doorway.

'You know you are always welcome.'

'You know I'm not,' she countered.

'Veronica. Come on,' I had said. 'What's this about?' But my phone had started ringing before she could reply.

That last Saturday all we did was fight. First when we took

the boys to the park. Then again that night, when it was only the two of us.

'Maya. What would you want Veronica to know if you could talk to her now?' Lucy asks, bringing me back to the present.

I remember how Veronica looked the last time I saw her. Standing in her front garden, her face lit a ghoulish white by a streetlight, her arms firm across her chest.

'I'm so sick of being second best.' That was the last thing she said to me.

I look at Lucy 'I'd say I'm sorry. I'm just so sorry. I wish that night never happened.'

Lucy nods. I can feel tears welling up that I won't be able to stop. I'm tired of crying. It's exhausting.

'If she were to hear you, what do you think she'd say back?'

Would she be angry at me? Would she still think I had let her down? Probably. She was so steeled in her will that I don't think death would change that.

'I don't know,' I whisper.

Lucy waits a moment, letting me get back in control of myself. 'You haven't mentioned the funeral. That was on Friday?'

I nod. 'Yeah, it was.'

'What was that like for you?'

'Hard. I sat at the back. I didn't want to see her mother.'

'Her mother. Why not?'

'I don't know what to say to her.'

She nods, crosses her legs and leans back into the upholstered armchair. 'You say you were close friends... for six years.'

I nod. We spent the first session talking about Veronica; how we met, what we used to do together. How our children grew up together. And how now I feel like I have a hole ripped in me. I'm not sure why she's going over the same details again.

Lucy looks at the clock that is behind my head on the wall. 'We're out of time. It would be great to see you again next Tuesday. We can talk about this more then. In the meantime, do you have friends in common with Veronica?'

'Of course. She knew a lot of people.'

'It could help to speak with someone who knew her. Share your good memories.'

I shake my head for no.

'Well, it doesn't have to be that. What about spending time with a friend outside of your family? Someone you get along with. I'm not saying that you shouldn't be sad... but a couple of hours of distraction might do you good. Being alone is the worst thing for you right now.'

When I thought about it, the times I had felt best over the last ten days had been when I was distracted. Playing a card game with the boys, a trashy TV show or a phone call with Isobel. I spent so much time with Veronica that I have few friendships left.

'There is an old friend I've reconnected with lately.'

'There you go. That's your homework for this week. I want you to make plans with them. Get a coffee or see a movie.'

'Okay.'

'It doesn't have to be about Veronica. But give yourself a break.'

12

ISOBEL

I never met Veronica Hayes, but she had been looking for me.

I'm still reeling from what Liam told me in the pub last night. I haven't slept.

'She didn't speak to me after we broke up. I tried. I tried hard, believe me...' Liam's voice had trailed off. 'She refused to speak to me for years. Then, out of the nowhere she called, she wanted to have a drink.'

'How long ago was this?'

'A year, maybe two.'

'What did she ask, Liam? How did she even know me?'

He looked over his shoulder. The pub was busy, but it was too loud for anyone to be paying attention to us. 'Where you were. If you had a family. If you were close with your parents. There were other things, but to be honest, I can't remember.'

'You remember that she asked though.'

'Well, it's unusual for your estranged ex-girlfriend to ask about your even more estranged ex-girlfriend,' he said with a shrug.

Why did she want to know about me so badly? A woman who once lived in the same town as her. Sure, we had a few friends in common, but that was not worth an obsession.

There is a passing physical resemblance. We both have long red hair, which is I suppose is eye catching. Hers is a shade darker than mine. It's petty to mention, but she's better looking than me. I have my father's angular cheekbones and long nose. Veronica was a classic beauty; full lips and hooded eyes.

I guess we could pass for sisters. But we're not. The only time we've ever been in contact is the day I found her. She was dead by then.

The light is creeping in from under the curtains of my bedroom. My mind is chasing itself around in circles.

I need to clear my head. I need to run.

It's been over a week since I've exercised. Running isn't a fitness thing for me. I mean, it's healthy and I'm sure the boost to my metabolism is helpful. It's more of a mind space thing. Moving meditation.

When I'm running, my brain thinks in a different way. It becomes more abstract. Maybe it's the sound of my feet on pavement, a constantly recurring pattern that affects brain waves like certain types of music do.

It gets me out of my head. I stop worrying about the small stuff, if only for forty-five minutes. With a bit of mental distance, I feel better. It's relaxing to do something so strenuous.

While I'm ready to run, I'm not ready to go back to the beach at the bottom of the cliffs. I don't know if I ever will be. I walk from my house to the nearest street corner; my idea of a warmup, but instead of heading towards the water, I turn and head back into town. There's some parkland beyond the shops. If I do a few laps then head home, it will be a good workout.

I break into a run, my feet quickly finding their rhythm on the concrete path. It's early and the air is still crisp. Soon it will be summer and we won't have these cold mornings any more.

It's only been a few minutes, but already I feel better. I shouldn't have waited so long to get back to running.

A low groan of an engine snaps my attention to the present. There's a car behind me. I catch it in my peripheral vision. At first, I don't pay attention. Two blocks on and it's still the same distance behind me. Maybe they're looking for an address or are lost. I keep running.

Taking a full glance behind me, I see that it's a four-wheel-drive. It's white, with blacked-out windows. Not an unusual choice of car around here. People like to surf and boat and caravan. Big cars are popular for their storage and ability to tow. But this doesn't look like a car that goes down the beach. It's spotless. It looks brand new. That's what makes it stand out. Who has a clean car near the beach?

After another block, I turn around again. It's still there. But now, instead of being a hundred metres behind me, it's only fifty. Pushing myself, I try to run a little faster. But I can hear the low mumble of the diesel engine getting closer and closer.

Could the car be following me? I remind myself that this is a small town and there's protection in that. Nobody tries anything because somebody is always watching. It's nothing, I tell myself.

The town is still asleep and there's no sound other than the murmur of the car and my feet on the concrete. And my breath; faster and faster.

The shops aren't far, less than a few hundred metres. I don't know if anything will be open this early, but it gives me a notion of safety. The car is closer again; it feels like it is right on my heels. My heart is beating fast, I can feel it pounding in the back of my throat.

In the corner of my eye, I can see the white vehicle only meters away. There's only a thin strip of brown grass between me and the road. It wouldn't be that hard for someone to get out of that car and attack me. Or worse, grab me and pull me inside.

I sprint, heading at full pelt towards the shops. I can see the row of low buildings. I don't know if I will make it. If they want me, they could take me.

I turn to the right; the car is beside me. The windows are tinted and I can't see who's inside. The car keeps moving forward at the same pace I run at.

The road I'm on ends at a T intersection. I can't see anyone around, but then I notice that the door to the milk bar is propped open. I turn left and sprint as hard as I can towards the open door. I turn back just for a second to see the car lulling at the intersection, watching me.

I burst through the half-open door, setting off a bell and startling a woman who is stacking up bottles in a fridge. I stop in the middle of the shop, doubling over and breathing hard. My elbows dig into my thighs.

Her eyebrows dart up. 'You must be in a rush for your milk this morning.'

'There was a car-' I start but then I stop myself. I don't want to sound crazy.

'You all right, love?' The woman stands. She's my mother's age, thin lipped with a tight perm. I don't know her.

'Yeah… it's okay. I've just forgotten my wallet.'

Through the shop window I see a flash of white as the car drives past. The hum of the engine decreases, and hopefully this means they're leaving and not coming back.

She shrugs and turns back to stock her refrigerator. Taking the cue, I leave.

I'm grateful she's an early starter. I take a few minutes out the front, leaning against the glass front of the shop. For all I know, that car is waiting around the corner for me.

I think about calling someone to pick me up, but who? My parents were still asleep and God knows they worry enough already. Maya Henry comes to mind, she's been kind. But she has her own family to worry about.

Instead of calling someone, I start walking home. The sun is creeping upwards on the horizon now and people and cars are beginning to fill the streets. Noises fill up the spaces that were empty before. The chirp of birds and the chatter of children in their front yards.

Normally I'd run the whole way, but I'm buggered after the sprint. My calf muscles are burning. Not a great way to come back after a break from exercise.

I rack my brain for who might want to scare me like that. Could it have been someone playing a joke? Bored teenagers? No. The car was too expensive for that. No one I knew drove anything like it. Now I didn't remember the make, let alone the number plate, so there is no way to tell if it was the same car I saw parked outside the pub. White four-wheel-drives are common.

Running broke me into a sweat, but by the time I reach home I'm cold. I slip my hand to the small of my back where the front door key is zipped inside an interior pocket. As I get to the front door, I see it's open. Only by a few inches, but definitely open. My stomach drops.

I always leave the front door locked when I run. I know I did this morning. It was locked from the inside, I pulled it shut. Or did I? Is there any chance I could have forgotten?

Standing on my concrete driveway, I'm frozen in place. Should I call the police? That sounded a little paranoid. What would I tell them? That I left my front door unlocked by accident and I want them to check it out for me? But that together with a strange car following me... I should call.

My phone was inside, still on my bedside table. Usually, I would take it with me on a run, but I had forgotten this morning. The house to the left was a holiday home, usually empty. My neighbours on the right leave for work early. If I wanted to call the cops, I needed to get upstairs first.

I tell myself I'm overreacting. If someone broke in, there'd be a sign of forced entry. A smashed window or a broken lock. And if someone had gotten inside, chances were they would have grabbed my laptop and jewellery and hightailed it out of here already.

Taking my chances, I push the door the rest of the way open and walk inside, leaving it open behind me. I look to my left, to the guest bedroom. Nothing is touched or upturned. The quilt is still smooth and the photo frames are lined up on top of the dresser. Thieves trash a place. They look through your drawers and make a mess.

Lightly, I tread up the staircase. The house is silent, all I can hear is the pad of my footsteps on timber. I reach the landing, standing close to the stairs in case I need to sprint back again.

I look to the front of the house and then the back, there's no one here. Everything is as I left it.

I think my mind is playing tricks on me.

To be certain, I go room to room. First to the kitchen and living room, then down the hallway, sticking my head into each of the unused bedrooms at the rear of the house. I even open the wardrobes. The study is empty, my laptop the only thing sitting on the long timber desk.

Was there really a car following me? Perhaps they were texting, driving too slow and not paying no attention to a solitary woman jogging on the footpath adjacent. I shook my head. No. I didn't imagine being followed. That was real.

I'm certain that no one has been inside. My shoulders drop and I let out a sigh of relief. The front door must have been unlocked the whole time I was out. Cursing myself for being so stupid, I walk in to my bedroom, looking forward to a hot shower.

Something catches my eye. I stop in the middle of the room. There's a newspaper on the bed. I never read newspapers and I would never buy one. Someone has brought it into the house. I feel myself freeze in place, but force myself to turn around. Was there someone still here?

The house is quiet. I listen for a footstep or a sound, something that would give away that I am not alone. There is only the dripping of the tap in the ensuite bathroom. Maybe they are already gone. But why a newspaper?

On shaky legs, I walk over to the bed. The covers are pulled tightly over the mattress neatly, like I left them this morning. In the centre is a newspaper folded in quarters.

I unfold the paper and then put it back down on the bed. The headline screams at me.

BODY ON THE BEACH: LOCAL BUSINESS WOMAN SLAUGHTERED.

In the picture, Veronica is smiling. It looks like she's actually smiling, not like in a posed photo, like someone caught her in the middle of a laugh. Her hair is out and falling in waves. I've never seen the picture before.

There's something else on the bed. A yellow post-it note. I pick it up between my thumb and forefinger. I feel sick. The sticky side is facing me, so I turn it towards myself to see a message scribbled in blue pen. There are only three words.

STOP ASKING QUESTIONS.

13

ISOBEL

I'm sitting at my kitchen table with a cup of tea that a police officer has made me. It's weird to have someone make me a drink in my own house.

Her name is Stacey Collins. I thought they might send a patrol car out, whoever was free. No, she tells me, she's on the case. She's come here especially for me, it appears.

They don't need to tell me they are Melbourne cops. Both of them hold themselves differently. They walk up my driveway more upright than a local cop would. They called me Miss Franco, the local cops would just call me 'love' or 'sweetheart'.

An ambulance came around too, but after a few minutes the paramedics left. I suppose it was a formality.

I've never changed the locks on any house I've lived in. I've got friends who do it as soon as they move in. I've never bothered. If someone wants to rob you, they're going to. It's not that hard to break into a house.

That wouldn't be so bad. If someone broke in and took my jewellery, my laptop. Whatever. They're insured. They can be replaced. This person wasn't after my stuff. They wanted to scare me. And they are damn good at picking locks.

'You want to call a locksmith?'

I nod. I'm going to do more than call a locksmith. This place is going to be full of sensors and security cameras as soon as I can get someone around to install them.

Stacey sits opposite me at the kitchen table. I don't know what time it is, but it's still morning. The light coming in through the back windows is still soft. She nods at her partner, directing him to leave. I hear his footsteps as he takes the stairs back down to the front door.

'So, you didn't know Veronica Hayes?' She takes a sip of her own tea, which she's helped herself to.

'No.' I look at my hands on the kitchen table, tracing the grain of the timber with my eyes. Why does any of this matter? I've already told the police this part.

'You didn't know her name? Or her face? Her photo is on a lot of For Sale boards around here.'

'I lived in Melbourne for a long time. I moved here two months ago.'

She nods. 'You grew up in Cape Cross though, right?'

'Yes. But I never met her. I never even heard her name.' I lift my gaze from the table to the windows across the back of the house. Why is she asking me questions she knows the answer to? Someone broke into my house. Isn't that the more pressing issue?

'You said that.' She opens a note pad in front of her and scribbles something. 'Did you know she had dealings with your grandfather?'

I didn't know that. I knew from Liam she had asked around about him and me. 'What kind of dealings?'

'From what I hear, she wanted to sell the quarry he owned.'

'The quarry? He sold that years ago. It was an off-market deal.'

He made most of his money from mining the quarry, long before I was born. It had made plenty of other people money too, keeping them in jobs for years. When there was no rock left, he sold off the land to a developer. I don't know anything else about it.

Stacey Collins flipped backwards through her notepad. 'It was four years ago. Two years before your grandfather died. And, according to Veronica's family, she brought the buyer to him.'

'She did?'

'Did your grandfather ever speak to you about that? About who bought the quarry?'

'No. We didn't... we didn't talk about things like that.'

'Things like that? Money?'

I nod.

We did though. He used to sit me down on a Wednesday after-noon. Every week, my father would drop me off there after school and pick me up before dinner. Dad never came inside, always waiting out the front for me. He never spoke a word to his father-in-law.

My grandfather taught me about compound interest and bad debt. He told me that if something is ever free, then you are the product. He lectured me on how I should live my life once I was an adult.

'You need a real profession,' he would often say.

'Psychology?' I said.

'The world doesn't need more head shrinkers. What about a doctor?'

'I'll never get in to medicine.'

'Not with that attitude,' he laughed. 'It's not the smartest that succeed. It's the ones who keep trying.'

It was him who later pushed me into law. He hired tutors for me when I was in my final year of school. He knew someone at the university. He lobbied them into accepting me and paid my fees upfront. Sometimes I wonder where I would have ended up if he hadn't done that.

Stacey Collins is waiting for me to comment. I'm not sure what she expects me to say.

'Was Veronica angry?' I ask.

'About the quarry? I don't know. Enough that people remember. Her family mentioned it right away.'

'Do they want the commission?' I ask.

'Their only daughter is dead. They've just taken over the care of their grandson. I don't think they give a shit about the money.' Stacey says, her voice deadpan.

'So, why are you asking me about my grandfather?' I say. 'What has any of this got to do with me?'

'You lived in the same town. She had business with your grandfather at least once. You must have at least known the same people.'

I sigh. She probably knew we had an ex in common too. Not to mention, a friend in common in Maya.

'It's a small town. But I never met her. Or heard of her. Or had anything to do with her before I saw her on that beach.'

She presses her lips into a fine line and looks at her notepad. 'So, what about you then? Do you have enemies?'

'Enemies? No.' There were certainly people who didn't like me by association. But that didn't count as an enemy.

'What about Benjamin Smith?'

'He's my ex.' His name still stings.

'A recent ex.' she adds, her gaze locked tightly on me.

'Yes.'

'Why did it end?'

I see where she is going with this. 'Ben didn't break into my house.'

Stacey raises her eyebrows. 'Sometimes people do things we don't expect. Things we don't think they're capable of. Especially when they're placed under stress.'

I shake my head at the suggestion. 'There's no malice between us. It ended. We are both fine with that.'

She seems to accept my answer.

'And what about Liam Goddard? What's your relationship there?'

'There is no relationship.'

Her eyes shoot up. My answer was too fast.

'He's not an ex-boyfriend as well?'

I swallow hard. 'An ex-boyfriend. Who I haven't seen in years.'

'You were seen drinking with him at the top pub last night.'

I sigh. 'Yeah. I ran into him. But there's no relationship.'

'Except when you hang out at the pub?' She raises her eyebrows again.

'For one drink.'

'What did you talk about? The good old days?'

Now I feel like she is mocking me. 'No. I offered my condolences. I was there less than an hour.'

'Condolences. Because Veronica is his ex-girlfriend?'

I shrug.

'You and Veronica have a lot in common for two people who never met.'

This time I don't say anything at all.

'Do you think that's strange?' asks Stacey.

'Yes.'

She's surprised. She was waiting for me to make an excuse. To tell her it was coincidence or the result of living in a small town. But I'm no fan of talking in circles. If she's going to accuse me of something she needs to come out and do it.

'I don't know why we have all these things in common. Or why someone followed me in their car. Or why someone is leaving threats in my bedroom. Isn't that your job?'

'We will look into it. In the meantime, change your locks. Today if possible. You could always stay with a friend.'

I nod.

'Someone not involved with all of this, I'd suggest. Stay away from the case. Stay away from anyone who had anything to do with Veronica. It's likely someone is trying to frighten you.'

'Okay.'

'That includes Liam Goddard.'

'What? Is Liam a suspect?'

She presses her lips together for a moment before she answers. 'If I were you, I'd keep my distance from him and his son.'

'His son?' Liam doesn't have children.

'I'm talking about Max Hayes. Liam is the father of Veronica's son.'

14

ISOBEL

Maya circles a spoon in her coffee. She's dressed in wide-legged navy pants and a loose cream top.

Her invitation had surprised me, but it wasn't unwelcome. She'd sent me a text the day after the police had been at my house. I'd spent most of the day at home, looking out the window, watching for a white four-wheel-drive. Anxiety has settled under my skin.

'You've got a beautiful place,' I say, as I cast my eyes around.

Maya's house is fit for its own Instagram feed. Everything matches everything. We sit on deep navy armchairs at the back of the house. The walls are a pale grey and the plush carpet is charcoal. There are perfectly framed family photos on the wall. Her twin boys wear blue shirts in the pictures, as if to match the decor in the room.

'That's a nice big house up on the cliffs you've got yourself.'

She's smiling, a look of glee in her eyes. 'Exactly how much money did your grandfather leave you?'

Her question is in jest and she doesn't expect me to answer. 'Not as much as everyone seems to think.'

She rolls her eyes. 'Your Mum must have pissed him off to get written out of the will.'

'I don't know what happened. They spoke to each other, but only a little. She would never visit him though; she still doesn't come around to the house now. My grandfather never approved of her marrying my father.'

'God, why can't someone leave me a house? I'm up to my eyeballs in debt with this place.'

It's not just the house he left me either. There's also a trust fund that matured this year, on my thirty-second birthday. I've never told anyone about it, not even Ben. To be honest, I'm not certain how much is in there. There's a lot of paperwork that arrived on my birthday that I need to sort out.

Maya isn't trying to be unkind, but I hate when people react like this. It makes me feel guilty for having something I didn't work for but I didn't ask for either. I wish no one in this town knew my business and I could just live my life.

'Anyway. I love your house,' I say. 'You'll have to come around to my place and give me some decorating tips.'

'Thanks,' she gives a small smile. 'We try to keep it nice. The boys are rough on it though. I feel like I'm cleaning up a lot of the time.'

'Are they at school today?'

'Yeah.' She nods. 'They're in their first year of primary school.'

The same age as Veronica's son. Who could be Liam's son as well. Was Stacey Collins telling me the truth?

'Maya, can I ask you a question?'

'Of course.' Her eyes meet mine.

'It's about Max.'

'Veronica's Max?' Her voice lowers. 'What about him?'

'Yes.' I nod. 'Is he Liam's son?'

Her eyebrows shoot upwards. 'Who told you that?'

'There was a cop at my house. Stacey Collins. She asked me a heap of questions about Veronica. And she claimed that Max was Liam's son. It was weird though. It was like she was trying to gauge my reaction when she said it.'

'That is weird. Why would she go out of her way to tell you that?' She looks past me, towards her kitchen. There's a sound at the front of the house.

'I don't know. It's not true?'

'No. It's true. But he hasn't been in Max's life for a few years.'

'Really?' It's a surprising revelation. When we dated, Liam used to talk about having kids all the time. He wanted a family. I can't imagine him not being in his child's life, no matter what the circumstances were.

Maya tilts her head to one side and takes a moment to consider it. 'By the time I became friends with Veronica, her relationship with Liam was strange.'

'Strange? So they were on bad terms?'

Maya shakes her head. 'When I first met Veronica, Max was a baby. They were together then, but Liam was stuck in Melbourne for work. He wanted her to move there, she wanted him to come here.'

'He didn't want to leave his career,' I say.

She shrugs. 'Something happened a couple of years in and they ended things. They didn't have much contact. She went out of her way to avoid him.'

'You think the distance got in the way?'

'She didn't like to talk about it.'

Maya reaches forward from the couch, placing her empty coffee cup on the table. She starts to speak again.

'I did wonder a lot about it. But I never knew if it was Max she was trying to keep away from Liam or herself. Anyway, why are you asking?' She leans back into the couch.

'No specific reason,' I say. 'Just the cops asking me questions. They're trying to figure out something.'

Her face falls. 'They're trying to figure out who hurt Veronica.'

'It doesn't seem like they're doing that in a direct way. They asked questions about people that don't matter.'

And they seem to think I know the answers to those questions.

'You said they came to your house? Did they tell you they were coming?'

I haven't mentioned the car following me or the newspaper on my bed. Instead of answering, I shrug the question off.

'Do you think Liam is a suspect?' I ask.

She shakes her head. 'There's been nothing between them for a long time.'

'Did she have a boyfriend?'

That gets a small smile out of her. 'No,' she answers.

Well, maybe it wasn't about love then. I push my only other lead.

'Did she tell you anything about her selling the quarry?'

'The police asked me that. I don't really remember much about that. She was a good person, but sometimes she could be stubborn. Especially with work stuff. She pissed a lot of people off. And people pissed her off as well.'

'That happened a lot?'

'I wouldn't say a lot. But once or twice a year she'd get into some kind of squabble or fight with someone. She didn't dwell on it. Not usually.' Maya was looking over my shoulder again. I couldn't tell if she was staring into the distance or waiting for her husband to walk in the door.

'Not usually?'

'She brought up your grandfather a few times after the fact. That whole thing with the quarry was a while ago. She did mention him to me recently. And she asked if I knew you.'

That's the second person Veronica asked about me.

'What did she want to know?'

'Where you were, mostly. I said you were working in Melbourne. That we were friends back in school. She asked if you had a good relationship with your grandfather and I said I had no idea.'

'Do you know why?'

'No. She often asked a lot about people. Knowing what was going on in town was part of her job. She hadn't mentioned the quarry in a long time. She was busy with something, a new project she mentioned.'

'What was the project?' I ask. Was there another bad deal she got mixed up in?

'You know that old hospital that got closed down years ago? Some developers were after it, wanting to build townhouses. Whoever owns it wanted to keep the whole thing quiet, so it was happening off the market.' She pauses for as a moment. 'I wonder if that will go through now.'

'Why would she keep it quiet? Wouldn't she want her name out there? That's how real estate agents get business.'

'The owner might have wanted it quiet.' Maya shrugs. 'You're really trying to figure this out?'

'When I saw her on the beach that morning, she reminded me of myself. It was... I guess it upset me. But now it feels like it's closer to me. Like she's not a stranger at all. I keep finding more coincidences. All these signs that our lives were linked.'

'Linked?'

'Linked is the wrong word. But we have all these things in common. I tried to stop thinking about it. As soon as I move on, something new comes into my path.'

'Who do you think did it then?' Maya asks. 'Do you have a theory?'

'I have no idea.'

She sighs. 'I'm not sure either. The police like Liam for it. I mean, it's the easiest target. It's always the disgruntled boyfriend. Maybe they're not looking at other options. They've put blinders on.'

'You don't think it was him?'

'No,' she says quickly. 'I don't. But if they've got nothing else, I can see why the police would be looking closely at him.'

'Maybe,' I nodded.

Maya walks over to the other side of the room where the television is switched off. It is positioned on a low-lying entertainment unit, with drawers for DVDs. She opens up one of the drawers and pulled out a thin, grey laptop.

'Take it,' she says, holding out the laptop to me.

She places it in my hands and I wait for an explanation.

'It's Veronica's.'

'You have her laptop?' I ask, surprised.

She nods.

'This needs to go to the police.'

'I don't trust them,' she says. 'I've been through it and there's nothing I can find. Unless I've missed something. You have good intentions. If I want her laptop in anyone's hands, it's yours.'

I nod. I decide to take it. I could look through it and then give it to the police, if I decided that was the right thing to do. Or not.

The sound of a loud crash and the slamming of a door echoes from the hallway. The excited chatter of children follows. I can see how this place could go from peaceful to disaster fast.

'Take your shoes off!' Maya calls, shaking her head.

'Mum!' calls a child's voice. 'Dad says we can have one treat from the jar.'

The echoes of footsteps tumble down the hallway. The two boys appear at the end of the couch. Both had the same dark blonde hair, left long but cut well.

'Where's Dad?' Maya asks.

'He's in the garage, he said he will be in soon.'

'David's been running the boys around for me the last week,' she says.

'It must be good to have him home with you,' I say.

She doesn't answer.

15

ISOBEL

When I slip my charger into the port of Veronica's laptop, it occurs to me that we even have the same computer. I spend the next two hours going through every file on a dead woman's laptop. I open the deleted items. Veronica used a MacBook. What some people don't realise is that you need to delete your deleted items. Otherwise, they'll just sit in the recycling bin for days. Or in my case, months.

My laptop sits on my desk, next to Veronica's. Hers is open and mine is closed. They are almost exactly the same model. Another weird coincidence to give me the creeps. Then again, who doesn't use a Mac these days?

It's weird to be thumbing my way through her life like this. Scouring search results and chatting to her ex-boyfriend was one thing. Going through her private correspondence is another.

So far, I've read some very boring work emails, pages of property ad copy, and clicked through the photos of houses she sold. Thinking she might be one of the few people left in the world who only use their laptop for work, I am about to give up.

I see the rubbish bin icon on the bottom of the right-hand side of the screen. If she was anything like most people, she never emptied it. When I open it, I find hundreds of files. After sorting by date, I scan each file name, looking for something relevant.

A folder named "hospital" catches my eye. There are plans of the old hospital, original floor plans. There is also a plan of a proposed development. Twenty-four modern townhouses. Close to the town centre and the beach, they could be worth a lot of money.

In a box in the left-hand corner of the plans is the name of the draftsman who had drawn up the townhouses. Beneath in neat square font: Client: V Hayes.

She had the plans drawn up herself. The deal she was trying to do was not for a client. She wanted to buy the site and develop it herself. Or did she already own it? She would need a lot of cash to get that together.

Her entire email folder is empty. That makes me think someone has deleted whatever was there. The only person with access was Maya. And she was the one who had volunteered the laptop to me. What would she be hiding?

I try the same trick again in the mail program, but the deleted folder is empty. A message pops up asking if I want to set up a new mail account. It's as if she'd never used this laptop to email anyone.

Which is a possibility. She probably had a work email address. A few years ago, the company I worked for moved their email to a web-based server. Instead of using the installed mail client on a computer, you use a web browser to retrieve your email from anywhere.

It takes a few tries to find it. Google Mail isn't set up. Then I try Outlook. It's not as popular as it used to be, but still worth a shot. I get lucky. Not only is it the right program, but her username and password are already saved.

Why haven't the police done this? They must be aware she had a laptop. Why aren't they looking for it? Was it possible she had a second work computer? Are they not looking hard enough?

There are only a handful of emails in the inbox, all work related, mentioning offers or inspections. There is nothing about the hospital. There is something in the draft folder. An email that was written by Veronica but not sent. The blank bar at the top shows no recipient.

Thank you for taking the time to meet with me last night. I know that the subject matter is delicate.

I appreciate that your client doesn't want to move forward without evidence. However, I believe that there are medical records in this regard that will clear up any doubts.

I will be able to forward these to you on Wednesday.

Veronica had stopped typing there. She might have planned to finish it later, or decided to not send it at all. There is no way of knowing. Either way, she had never sent it.

Wednesday. I look at the draft date and then open it on her calendar. It's the Wednesday before she died. There was only one appointment scheduled that day. Nine am at the old hospital. There was no name or phone number attached like her other appointments.

A medical record. There couldn't be any documents left at the old hospital though. The place had been shut down for years. Anything like that would have been moved to a storage facility, especially sensitive information.

Veronica would have been there only a few days before she died. Whatever the 'delicate subject' was, her evidence could have been inside that hospital.

There's only one way to find out. I guess I'm going to the old hospital.

16

MAYA

I have an idea, but I don't dwell on it. If I do, I'll talk myself out of going. When I get out of the car, I know this is a mistake. She's not going to want to see me. But I walk across a row of pavers that divides a rose garden and I ring Heather Hayes' doorbell anyway.

This idea felt less crazy in the middle of a sleepless night. It occurred to me Heather is the one I should be talking to. If there's another soul that's mourning the loss of Veronica, it must be her. I should have come here sooner.

The other side of the argument is that she likely doesn't want to see me, or anyone. She was hostile before this happened. She could be flat out aggressive now.

I hear Veronica's name spoken in the streets each day, but no one actually talks about her. Not who she was as a person or what she did. She was a mother who gave out hugs and a friend who lent an ear. They say her name, but only talk about how she died and where she was found. And what she might have done to deserve what happened to her.

She used to be a person, now she's a victim. She's that picture stuck to every news story. I'm not sure where it came from, but now it's the one that gets flashed on the front of the news websites. Veronica has become a construct.

No matter why she died or how, her death is an injustice. Someone's mother and someone's daughter is lost to them. Someone's life ended too soon. I want to undo it. I want that wrongness to ebb away like an outgoing tide.

Sad is a two-dimensional description. People know I'm sad, but not the rest of the dark rainbow that makes up my emotions. I feel cheated, uneasy and also full of dread that this isn't over yet. I've been left alone with all of it. David is avoiding me. Lucy listens but gives no solutions.

So I find myself here, outside an average-looking house in an average part of town. Brick veneer, tiled roof. Two large windows facing the street. A tidy garden with shrubs and roses. The roses are not average, they're quite spectacular.

Heather opens the door. Her brown eyes are too large for her face and her cheeks are sunken. She's not been sleeping either. She gives me a look over, her hand still on the brass doorknob. I'm worried she's going to close it on my face.

'Hi,' I say. I suck in a deep breath of air as I wait for her reaction.

'Maya,' she takes a step back and opens the door for me. 'Did you come to see Max?'

I didn't and I immediately feel guilty. 'Is he home?'

'No.' She shakes her head slowly. 'Back at school now. I thought that was best.'

'Yes,' I say. 'I wanted to drop by and see how you were doing.'

'As well as can be expected,' she says, turning around. She walks ahead, leaving the door open for me to follow her.

Inside, the house is all original. Everything looks the same as it would have twenty years ago. It's impeccably neat. I take a seat on the black leather couch, the newest-looking thing in the house, and wait for Heather to do the same. Instead, she walks straight past me to an ironing board set up in the corner of the lounge room.

She doesn't speak, instead she switches the iron back on, casting a look of disdain to the twisted lump of clothes in a washing basket beside her. Only now to I notice the neat piles of clothes on the buffet along the wall.

'Is it washing day?' I ask, more to start a conversation than anything.

She looks up, squints slightly, then shakes her head. 'Oh, no. I'm just getting through Veronica's things.'

'They're Veronica's clothes?'

'Yes. This is the last lot. I've washed them all and put them back in her bedroom.' She states this in a matter-of-fact tone.

'Right. That must be awful, having to go through her things.'

'Well, yes. But we got through it in a day, Neil and I. We brought across all of Max's things and set them up in the spare room for him. When I was in her house, I realised I couldn't leave her things there. It felt like I was leaving her there. So it's all in her bedroom.'

I don't think it's been her bedroom for a long time, but I nod in agreement, anyway.

'How is Neil?' I ask.

She shrugs. 'Back at work now.' Her big eyes are glassy and there's something vacant about her expression.

'I miss her a lot,' I say after a long silence.

She nods as if I have stated the obvious, but she says nothing. I think this may not be the right person for me to be talking to at all. I should go. I'm about to stand, but Heather starts talking.

'I keep buying Tim Tams.'

'What?'

'She loves them. No one else here eats them, but they were her favourite. Every time I walk past them in the supermarket, I pick up a pack. I can't stop myself.'

'Oh.'

'There's six packets in the cupboard now.'

I nod. It's strange, but is it any stranger than me wearing the ring she bought me every day, or reading the novel she lent me? I watch her return to ironing, almost manic. Perhaps her mental state is not so good.

'I should leave you to it,' I say. 'I wanted you to know that I'm thinking of you. And that I haven't forgotten Veronica.'

I stand up. She nods, her lips pressed firmly together. She doesn't move away from her ironing. I guess I'll let myself out.

'Take care of yourself then,' she says.

'You too.'

'And keep yourself out of Veronica's troubles.'

I freeze on the spot. 'What troubles?'

As she places the iron on its side she puts a hand on her hip. 'Well, it wasn't random, was it? Someone did it to her. She was always... getting into things.'

'Things?'

'Well, I don't know the half of what she was doing. But she was planning something. Said it would change her life.'

My stomach drops and my voice comes out flat. 'Change how?'

'She never told me. Sometimes she got excited over nothing,

about things that didn't end up happening. She was always like that. Even as a little girl.'

'And you think this was something bad?'

'How else could this happen to her? But you need to keep out of it, Maya. I'm not sure what it was, but steer clear.'

I nod. 'I'll see you soon, Heather.'

'And I saw you with Isobel Franco at Veronica's funeral. Keep away from her too.'

'Isobel? Why?'

'She's trouble.'

'Okay.' I can't tell if what she is saying is real or if it's paranoia speaking. Her ironing Veronica's clothes along with these strange accusations have me worried about her. 'Talk soon, okay? Do you have my number? You can call me anytime.'

'Yes. I think I do,' she nods.

Before I get to the front door, she calls out again. 'I mean what I said about Isobel. They're not a good family. The father has a history. I've been finding out all about it. Very dark stuff.'

17

ISOBEL

I'm not the first person to break into the old hospital, judging by the broken glass and misplaced plywood. Getting in is the easy part. It's when I'm inside that everything starts to go wrong.

The last time I was inside this hospital, I was a kid. From time to time, I drive past, but the gardens out the front are overgrown, and it's hard to see much.

The car park was still there and wide open. Of course, there aren't any cars. The hospital is a double-story dark-brick building, built in the seventies. The window frames are mission brown and the roof is flat. Most of the windows and doors have been covered with plywood sheets. I've brought a crowbar, a hammer, and some other tools from my father's shed. I hope he doesn't miss them before I get them back.

It turns out I don't need to get the tools out of the boot. As I walk to the back of the building, I see sheets of plywood discarded on the ground. As I get closer, I can see someone else has been here first, ripping off the plywood and leaving me an opening.

It doesn't take long to find an open space low enough to the ground. The lowest part of the window is below my knees, but the gap isn't much bigger than me. I think I can drop through legs first and land on my feet.

I'm careful as I ease myself through, looking out for shards of broken glass. It takes a few minutes, but I carefully navigate the gap without hurting myself.

I think this is the basement. I stop, and for a few minutes I listen. I want to make sure I am alone. There's nothing at all to hear. Not even the rustle of paper or the hum of a machine. If someone broke in here, they're long gone.

There is no electricity, and barely enough light inside for me to see. The grey linoleum floor is cracked in places. Dirt and leaves from the outside have blown in and are scattered across the floor. As I start walking through the corridors and looking through each room, I'm surprised to find furniture. I would expect it to have been sold off and the place emptied years ago. Visitors' chairs, desks, and even beds are still in place. Whoever was in charge of the shutdown did a terrible job.

If there's a records room, it's likely to be here in this basement. There was little trace left of the hospital online, let alone a floor plan. The documents on Veronica's computer gave me a site plan, but this showed only the dimensions of the land and the position of the building.

I push through a set of heavy steel doors that lead to a staircase going deeper. It gets darker as I descend. The smell of mildew filters through the air. Again, I stop and listen for a few minutes, making sure I am still alone.

At the bottom of the stairs, I find myself in another corridor. Pulling the torch I've brought out of my pocket, I flick it on as I make my way further into the darkness. The first door I open leads to a large, sparse room. The high glass windows sit at ground level outside provide little ventilation or light. I can still see more shards of glass, pushed inwards on the floor.

The next door is timber and painted beige. There's a padlock, but it was bust open long before I got here. I push the door open and let myself in. Piles and piles of archive boxes tell me I am in the right place.

Metal shelving is fitted around the perimeter of the room, with stacked boxes from the floor to the ceiling. There is an index stuck to each box, but no order in how they are stacked. 'Intake - April - 1985' is beside 'Purchase orders - IT Department.' Either they had a terrible administration team or these boxes have been moved around a hell of a lot.

One box is on the ground. 'Plans and permits' is written in thick black marker on its side. Could this have been what Veronica came looking for?

Kneeling on the ground, I pull the lid off the box. Inside are blueprints and plans of the hospital. I fold them outwards, I guess they are the original drawings by the architect who designed the place. I pull out more paperwork. There are similar documents, some of them with council permits. They are old. Older than me and older than Veronica.

At the bottom of the box is a smaller piece of paper. At first, I think it's a packaging slip. But I look closer; it's a birth certificate. It's Veronica's birth certificate.

There are more medical documents, all of them Veronica's. Someone had put it all in this box, underneath the plans. Had Veronica come here looking for information about the hospital or herself? Was it something more personal than a business deal gone bad? And why put them under all these other documents?

A large clatter outside of the storage room brings me back to reality. I drop Veronica's birth certificate; the paper floats to the floor. I hear the low creak of a heavy door opening followed by slow footsteps. Someone is coming down the stairs to the basement.

Nausea fills up my stomach. Are they looking for the same documents I am? Or are they looking for me?

Whoever is here, I don't want to cross paths with them. With all my focus on getting into this place and what I might find, I haven't considered how I'm going to get out. Or who else might be here.

If there's a second way out, I need to find it. Fast. I can hear their footsteps echo in the empty corridor. They're getting closer.

With the hope that the darkness will hide my movement, I slip out of the storage room. I keep my steps slow and quiet and my body close to the cold concrete walls.

I make my way down the corridor, away from the sound of footsteps. At its end, I can make out another door. I try to open it, but the handle doesn't turn. In desperation, I shove the full weight of my body against it. It doesn't help. The thing isn't going to budge.

Has the noise given me away? I strain my eyes searching the darkness. A shadowy figure disappears into one of the rooms of the corridor, then reappears a minute later. They are searching each room, one at a time, like I was doing not so long ago. I haven't got long until they find me.

My last attempt, I slam my shoulder into the door with the full force of my weight. It gives a small creak then gives. Another shove and it opens, a loud groan vibrating down the whole corridor. I slip through the small opening created, just as I see the shadow come out of the storage room. They've heard me.

This new room has more light, with a row of high windows meeting the ground level outside. Again, most of them have been smashed in and the floor is covered with glass. The floor and the walls are covered with linoleum and there is a row of steel compartment lockers along one wall. I'm in the morgue. There's no second door in this room. I'm stuck in here.

This room is a dead end. Appropriate for a morgue, right? I try to slow my breathing using force of will.

Footsteps approach from outside. I wait for them to fade, but they don't. The door creaks open. I hold my breath. The shape of a man fills the doorway and I turn and run for the furthest corner of the room.

But I don't make it there. Something gives in my ankle, I tumble forward. A sound comes out of me that is something like a scream. I skid onto the floor covered with jagged crystals of broken glass. The pain barely registers under the weight of fear.

I scramble forward as far as I can on my hands and knees. One of my arms is bleeding and I don't think I can defend myself. I'll have to try. I turn around to face my attacker.

'Izzy?' Liam Goddard stands in the centre of the morgue, his eyes wide and his face covered in sweat.

18

ISOBEL

The first thing Liam does is rip his shirt off. I am crouched on the ground, pressing my forearm to my chest. When I move, I hear broken glass crunch under my feet.

'What the hell are you doing here?' I blurt out.

I'm still afraid, but he looks even more surprised than I am. Liam's eyes go straight to my forearm. The blood has soaked through the fabric of my shirt and my chest and stomach are wet with it.

His shirt is in his hands when he kneels down in front of me. There's another crunch of glass, if he's not careful, he'll end up cut as well. He's wearing jeans, hopefully the denim is thick. His shirt is gone, but he has a black t-shirt on.

'Liam, why are you here?' I repeat.

He's only looking at my arms. In a short motion, he rips the fabric into two.

'Give me your arm.' He holds his hand out.

'Are you going to explain yourself?'

'Maybe once you stop bleeding,' He still doesn't look me in the eyes. He wraps one piece of what used to be his shirt firmly around my arm, then uses the second piece to tie a knot. 'Or you could tell me why you're in a disused morgue rolling around in broken glass?'

He stands up and I hear tiny crystals of glass falling to the floor.

'I'm looking for something,' I answer. I stand up too, I don't like being looked down on. As my legs straighten I feel dizzy, but it passes. Instinctively, I hold my arm to my chest.

'You're going to need a real hospital to get that fixed up.'

I nod.

'So, what are you looking for?' he presses.

'Honestly, I'm not sure. I... I knew that record room was there. And that it was still full of paperwork.'

'Yeah, I'd say given the state of it that a few people know it's there. You and I weren't the first people to go looking.'

'No. Did you find what you were looking for?'

He puts his hands on his hips. 'No.'

'What was it?'

He takes a step back, his weight moving on to his heel. 'You tell me yours and I'll tell you mine.'

For a moment, I pause. I have to make a decision whether I should trust him.

'I've got Veronica Hayes's laptop. I found a heap of documents on there, some of them relating to this site.'

Liam nods, waiting for me to say more.

'I found a box of documents in that storage room, but it wasn't all about the hospital. Perhaps she came to look for that but found something else.'

He raises his eyebrows. It isn't the answer he expected. 'And what, you think you're going to finish whatever she started? Find whatever mystery documents she was looking for?'

I nod. 'It sounds crazy, but it's all I've got.'

'All you've got? What are you talking about, Isobel?' Liam looks as confused as ever. I take a step closer.

'This all has something to do with me. Someone's been following me.'

'Who?' He waits for my answer, blinking.

I shrug. 'I don't know.'

He shakes his head. 'You've got to let the cops do their job. Not much point in knowing what Veronica was up to if you end up dead too.'

'What if the cops are trying to pin it on someone? Like me. Or my Dad. It's as if they don't want to consider anything else.'

'Anything else? What, like the fact they've dragged me in to be interviewed twice now? It was three hours the first time and five the second. Have you considered that your father isn't the only one who is under suspicion?'

'So that's what you're doing here? Trying to clear your name?'

He doesn't answer.

'Liam, tell me. I just told you why I'm here. I trusted you. Now you trust me.'

'Alright. A couple of years ago, I heard that this place was never cleared out. There were still records in here.'

'So, this is about Veronica then,' I say.

He sighs, and his arms drop back to his sides. 'Not really. I'm looking for a birth certificate. Max Hayes's birth certificate.'

'You're his father.' My voice is quieter than I expect it to be.

He nods. 'That's what Veronica told me. When he was born. But then a few years ago when she stopped talking to me... well, she wouldn't let me see him anymore.'

'So why do you need the birth certificate? He's with Veronica's mother. I'm sure you can see him. Work something out.'

He hesitates again. 'Her parents won't let me see Max. They're saying I'm not the father.'

'What? Didn't Veronica tell them? Or do they not want you around?'

He shrugs. 'I don't know, Iz. Everything is weird at the moment. It was okay at the funeral. Then they asked me for some space. At first, I thought they wanted some time for Max to come to terms with things. But then Heather told me to stay away. She won't respond to calls or messages.'

I take a moment to consider what Liam had said. Why would Veronica's parents shut him out?

'Heather's always been difficult. But now she's...' he hesitates. 'More extreme. I'm going to need legal help. That means documentation.'

'Did you find it?' I asked. 'Max's birth certificate?'

'No. I've never seen it.'

'But you're his father.'

Another thought occurs to me. Could Veronica's parents think Liam killed her? Had the police given them that impression? It made sense that they would shut him out like that if they did.

Liam breaks the silence. 'We need to get you to an actual hospital. You're going to need stitches.'

'I'll go,' I said, moving past him towards the metal door.

He shakes his head, 'I'm taking you.'

I shrug. I'm not going to be able to drive, anyway. I'll have to come back for my car later.

'Can you do me a favour though, Iz?'

'Depends on what it is,' I say, though I'm not really in a position to negotiate. I'm close to bleeding through this makeshift bandage on my arm.

'Don't tell anyone I was here.'

19

MAYA

The house is my project but I can let it become my prison. It was a dud when it was listed for sale. No one would go near it. It sat on the market for months, a deceased estate. The weatherboards were flaking paint, rotted in some places. The roof sagged in all the wrong places. Inside, the walls were nicotine yellow.

I saw through all that. I imagined the outside repainted in a pale blue, the timber windows white, the wraparound veranda restored and oiled. David could polish the floorboards, we could fix the walls and the sad, heaving roof. The picture I had in my mind is almost identical to the way the house looks today.

I was pregnant when we bought it. Neither David nor I knew if getting married was the right thing to do. I know we felt too young to be buying a house and having kids, but we never admitted it to each other.

It's long completed but the perfectionist in me always sees a project; a laundry cabinet that squeaks and doesn't close square. A plant that barely makes it through summer that doesn't suit. And the cleaning, there is always so much cleaning. I can't sit down with a cup of tea until I know that everything is away where it should be and free of dirt and dust. Which is almost never.

Sometimes it's more relaxing to be out of the house than in it. Tuesdays, I shop with Dad, and then see him again later in the week. Other days I do yoga or walk for a while down at Safety Beach. I used to have coffee with Veronica whenever she had the time.

Yesterday, I went and saw Heather. This morning, I took Dad to the doctors. By the time I pull up in my own driveway and press the button on the garage remote, it's almost noon. I glance at the clock in the car as I push it into park. There's a few hours before school pickup. That time will go quickly.

I walk into the entry and feel that something is not right. David's keys are on the hall table. They rest on the glass top, not in the small wooden bowl where they belong. He never comes home in the middle of the day. Work is always too busy.

'David?' I call.

He doesn't answer, but I hear a low scrape, the sound of the wrought iron kitchen stools on the tiled floor.

'Are you home?' He still doesn't respond.

I slip my shoes off and walk barefoot down the hallway. My shoulders have stiffened and something doesn't feel right. I shake it off, reminding myself that it's only my husband come home for lunch.

When I walk into the open-plan kitchen, he's sitting at one of the stools facing the marbled grey bench top. Exactly as I thought he would be. He doesn't look up. Instead, he looks down at a bowl of cereal he's made himself. His work clothes are covered in white dust. Normally I'd ask him to shower, but there's something strange about him today.

'David, why are you home? I just called out to you, didn't you hear?'

Only now does he look at me. He takes a moment before he speaks, slowly chewing and swallowing his cereal.

'Just checking in. Checking that you're alright. I expected you'd be home,' he answers.

I wasn't sure until now, but I can tell what's happening. It's happened like this before.

There's a part of me that wants to tell him where to go. That it's none of his business where I go and what I do. But there's a bigger part of me that hates a fight and will do anything to escape conflict.

'Dad had the doctors today,' I say.

'I know,' he nods. 'I called to check.'

I open my mouth, then I falter. He called the doctor? Was he trying to catch me in a lie? 'Why would you do that?'

'I came home for lunch yesterday and you weren't here either.'

He doesn't give me a chance to respond. 'Remember that night?' That party where the fight broke out? I said then that Veronica was bad news. That she's a person who brings trouble. You didn't listen then and you still don't now.'

Yes, I remember that night. Veronica's birthday, she was turning twenty-eight. The boys were two; it was one of the first times we left them with a babysitter.

'You were drunk that night,' my voice is a whisper. 'You don't remember what happened.'

'You were always different around her.'

I was happy around her. Veronica was dating Liam back then. I say dating, but I'm not sure what it was. They saw each other some weekends. He was talking about moving back, but she admitted to me she wasn't keen on the idea.

She'd invited a group of people to a bar. Maybe ten or twelve, not a big event, but it started going off the rails after midnight. David never danced. He stood at the bar chatting with a man who looked vaguely familiar. They might have played footy together.

How much had I had to drink? Too much. But it was fun, and I never got a night off like that. Veronica and I were dancing, spinning in circles, laughing loudly. One guy she worked with walked past and we grabbed him, pulling him between us.

I laughed harder until I felt a strong grip on my arm. David stood behind me.

'We need to go,' he had said.

Underestimating the seriousness of his tone, I stuck out my bottom lip. 'Oh, not yet.'

He leaned in toward me, pulling me away from Veronica at the same time. 'You're behaving like an idiot,' he hissed, his breath sour with alcohol. 'It's time to go home.'

His voice sobered me faster than a slap in the face.

'Go home then,' I said, raising my eyebrows in challenge. It was not how I spoke to anyone, especially David.

His hand wrapped around my arm; his fingers dug into my skin causing a flush of pain. With force, he pulled me toward him, away from Veronica.

'Hey!' Veronica said. 'Lay off her!' Her shouts drew the attention of everyone in the bar who was not already looking. David let go of my arm. Veronica reached out for my hand. I took it, she pulled me towards her.

'Get your nose out of it,' he sneered at Veronica. 'You're always in our business, you are. Always in someone else's business.'

'Calm down,' I said. I may as well have been talking to a wall. David's face was flushed red. Veronica looked like she could spit venom. And I'd taken her hand; I'd taken her side.

David turned and stormed out. For a moment, the bar was silent and the place felt like a vacuum. A few seconds passed, then the room whirred back into life again. That was when Liam appeared by Veronica's side. Where had he been this whole time? The expression on Veronica's face suggested she had noted his absence.

When Lucy asked me if David was violent, I said no. And I was telling the truth. It was only that one time. Grabbing at someone is not like punching. There was barely a bruise. He was drunk and I was being unfair.

Now he is sitting in the kitchen, and I can feel the same sensations. Something like that night. This time we are both sober. How long had this been brewing?

David spoons another bite of cereal into his mouth. 'Going to tell me where you were?'

'I just did. I was with Dad.' I put my handbag on the kitchen bench. I don't sit down.

'And what about yesterday?'

'What?'

'I came home yesterday. You weren't here,' he says.

'I was at yoga, David.' The lie comes off my tongue easily. I have done nothing wrong visiting Heather. But if he finds out, he will be angry.

He tilts his head to one side, as if he is considering whether he should believe me. 'Someone from work saw you driving. But you were on the other side of town. Nowhere near the yoga studio.'

Heather lived on the opposite side of town to us, what other reason could I have? I try to think fast. 'Just collecting my thoughts. Driving down by the water.'

It's not much, but it's the best that I come up with. Anyhow, I don't see why I should have to justify my own movements.

'Just wasting petrol, hey?'

I shrug. 'It's been hard. I don't feel like myself.'

'You don't act much like it either. But you haven't for a while.'

I straighten my spine and stand to face him. 'What's that supposed to mean?'

'You haven't been yourself in months.' His tone is flat, but there's an accusation underneath it.

I bite the inside of my mouth. What's there to say to that?

David is the first to speak. 'I never liked her, Maya. Now she's dead, and she's still getting you into trouble.'

'I'm not in trouble.'

'You're bringing trouble to us. You went to Heather Hayes' house.'

Then why didn't he say so? Instead, he's playing a twisted

game. 'I need someone to talk to. And you haven't been open on the subject.'

'I took you to a therapist.'

'I needed someone who was close to Veronica. Who misses her.'

'Oh, come on!' He shouts, slamming his hand on the bench top. The sound vibrates through the room.

He's so steady all the time, when he snaps like this it's frightening. But I won't let myself back down, even though it's the smart things to do.

'What? I'm not allowed to be sad? I don't get to grieve? All I get to be is a mother and a daughter and wife. No room for anything else, right?'

'That's just it, Maya. She was a mate. Sure, you're upset. But your kid didn't die. Not your parent or your husband. Just a friend. And yeah, you have an obligation to us. Go to therapy if you're sad. Talk to someone. But you can't go hanging around with her family. There are cops all over it. They've got a team from Melbourne. I hear they're dying to put it on someone. Anyone.' His voice is still raised, bouncing off the high ceilings.

'What are you taking about, David? I've spoken to the police already.'

'Exactly. They're watching you. They're watching me.'

'So what? I had nothing to do with it.'

He says nothing. His eyes fix on the grey swirl of the marble bench top. Then I realise why he's upset. I had nothing to do with it. But did he?

'David, who are you worried about? Me or you?'

His eyes narrow. He doesn't hesitate. 'I had nothing to do with her dying.'

Could he have hurt Veronica? My instincts say no. Then I remember that night, the way he grabbed me and pulled me away from her. Maybe my instincts aren't so great.

Both Veronica and David did a good job of avoiding each other for the four years after that party. They barely mentioned the other's name. On the last night of her life, when I went to meet Veronica, David had tried to call me. More than once. He'd messaged me, asking where I was.

Did he know I was with her? Did that old jealousy and rage from all those years ago resurface? Is he the person who sent Veronica to her death that night?

20

ISOBEL

'So, all of this came from a broken window?'

The doctor looks from me, to my deeply gashed arm, and then to Liam.

'Yes, I was trying to clean up some broken glass and I slipped over,' I lie.

The doctor knows I'm lying. She nods, but she doesn't meet my eyes. There is a quick glance to the nurse that's beside her. He disappears out of the room.

Why are they so suspicious? It's not like I came in with bullet wounds.

The hospital at Waringal has a good reputation. It's oddly calm in here. The walls are a faded green. Disinfectant stings my nose. There are doctors in Cape Cross. It would have been easier to go there than drive the forty minutes to Waringal. But Liam insisted.

'You'll wait two hours, pay too much and get a messy job with a bad scar,' he had said.

He was right, at least about the wait time. Since the old hospital had been closed, the local doctors had been under pressure. And while any treatment in a hospital was paid for by the government, a doctor in a clinic would give me a large bill. I can't speak to the quality of their stitches. I've never needed them before.

The triage nurse at the hospital sent me into a private room. Within fifteen minutes, a doctor had come in to stitch up my arm. While I told them I had broken it on glass, I had lied and said it happened at my home.

'It's shallow,' says the doctor. 'You'll have a scar, but it will fade.'

I nod.

With a swish of the white privacy curtain, the nurse comes back into the room. He smiles a lot. I don't think I'd be smiling so much if I worked in a hospital.

The triage nurse looks straight at Liam, who is leaning against the wall. 'Sir, could I borrow you for five minutes?'

He raises his eyebrows. 'What for?'

He smiles even wider. 'I need a Medicare form filled out for

Isobel. I was hoping you could help since she's out of action right now.'

Liam stands straight, lifting his weight from the wall. 'I'm just a friend.'

'Yes, that's fine.'

He looks confused, but follows him out of the room.

'Sorry this is taking so long,' the doctor apologises. 'There's glass inside the wound.' She pulls a piece out of my arm with tweezers and drops it into a plastic specimen container. 'I think that's the last one.'

I grit my teeth and wait for her to stitch. My eyes turn towards the green of the wall, I didn't want to watch.

The doctor doesn't start. Instead, she speaks. 'So, he's a friend?'

'Yeah.'

'Are you in any danger?' Her tone is blunt.

'What kind of danger? From Liam?' I'm surprised. My arm is cradled in one of her hands. 'No.'

'Okay. It's our policy to check when people come in with injuries like yours. If you are, there's people here who can help.'

I nod. 'It's fine. It really was just an accident. My Mum's been through the same thing plenty of times. It's fine. It's your duty to ask.'

'Your Mum's in here a lot?' Concern grips her face. I was doing a good job of raising red flags today.

I nod. 'She has brittle bone disease. So, if she's not here for her latest fracture, she's over the road in the specialist rooms seeing a doctor.'

'Right. Sorry to hear that. I probably know her if she's here that often.' She looks across at my chart. 'You have the same surname?'

I nod. The doctor smiles. 'Is your mother Jennifer Franco?'

'Yep.'

The doctor shifts her gaze to my arm and stars stitching. I look away.

'Unusual surname. She stayed for a while a couple of years ago. I remember her well.'

I nod. She has a good memory. 'That would have been when she was first diagnosed.'

'And what about you? I see nothing on your chart, so I'm guessing you came up negative?'

'Negative to what?'

There's a strange pause. 'Brittle bone is hereditary. It's standard practise for you to be tested.'

'I never have been. Mum never mentioned anything. I didn't know it was genetic.'

The doctor takes a deep breath. 'Your Mum would have got a

letter and a referral to give you. Sometimes family members don't pass them on… it sounds strange to us but sometimes they feel guilty for passing on a disease. Not that it's something anyone controls. It's a common reaction.'

My Mum wasn't like that. She was a straightforward woman, and if I could have an illness, she would never keep it from me. There had to be another explanation.

'Could she have a type that isn't passed on?'

The doctor shakes her head. 'Sometimes parents want to protect their children. Even when it makes little sense.'

The doctor put her tools down on the small table to one side of her. 'Before you go, I can get a referral letter for you. You don't have to get tested if you don't want to. You'll see a genetic counsellor first. But now you'll have the option.'

I thank her. If it's true, I don't understand why my mother wouldn't tell me.

'I'm finished, but take a few minutes if you need to. Give me ten minutes and I'll have the referral ready to go.'

'Thanks.'

She gives a small smile and leaves the room. I go to stand straight away, but feel a pull in my stomach. Waiting a few minutes is a good idea. After those stitches and that revelation, I feel a little giddy.

After ten minutes, I go back to the triage nurse at reception. Like the doctor had promised me, the referral was there. Liam sits on an olive-green plastic chair, hands clasped, staring at his feet. I call out to get his attention.

'Come on, let's go,' I say.

'Sorry, Iz. They wouldn't let me back in.'

'Yeah,' I grin. 'They were making sure you weren't my abusive boyfriend.'

'Oh. I didn't think of that.'

'Yeah, but that's 'cause you don't go around beating up on women.'

As he walks through the automatic doors, I see him grimace. I don't think he appreciates my humour.

I shrug it off. Liam holds open the passenger door and I sit down in his car.

Liam drives a hatchback, the same model as my car but a few years older. It was surprising. When we were younger, I always thought he would have ended up as a wealthy doctor or something. Now he is in his thirties and working in a bar.

'Hang on, I'll help you with the seat belt,' he calls as he turns around the back of the car to get in the driver's side.

'It's fine.' I manage with my good arm.

Liam sits down in the driver's seat and lets out a huff. 'You really haven't changed.'

'From what?'

'You don't let anyone help you.' He turns the key in the ignition and the engine tumbles into life.

'You have,' I say.

'What? Changed?'

'Yeah,' I say. 'You used to be so serious. You were all about your grades and what uni you were going to.'

He looks over his shoulder as he reverses. 'There was a lot of pressure on us. Our cohort, that is. What were we, class of 2004?'

'Yep. What kind of pressure?'

'Pressure to be successful. And a thin definition of what that meant. A university degree out of school. A corporate job by twenty-one. Then a house by twenty-five.'

I nod. 'That's kind of what I did,' I say. I catch my reflection in the mirror. I look tired.

'Do you think it was the right thing? I know you have a house, but do you think things could be different?' He merges the car on to the highway that leads led back to Cape Cross.

'If I didn't go to university?'

'If you didn't do what people expected you to. What your parents expected.' His eyes stay on the road.

'My parents are laid back. It was my grandfather that was the problem.'

'And if he wasn't in your life, what would you have done?'

I sighed. 'I'm not sure. Back at school, I liked psychology. Or teaching. Who knows? I might have changed my mind once I got to uni and ended up in law. Maybe the same things would have happened, anyway.'

It sounds like he had been thinking about this a lot. I'd had a couple of friends like that over the years. They worked hard for the ten years after school, then had some kind of early midlife crisis and packed everything in. Quit their jobs, lived in a van.

'You don't have any regrets?' He asks, still not looking at me.

I hesitate. 'I would have had children. Right away, in my early twenties.'

'Really?' He turns his gaze from the road and his eyes met mine for a second. 'I would have never picked that, Iz.'

'Me and kids? Am I really not that maternal?' I smile.

'No. You having kids that early. You always seemed happy to be working. Is that why you came back? You want a family?'

'No. I mean, yes. There was a rough plan around that. But it's not going to work out.'

'Is this the boyfriend you left in Melbourne?'

'You know about him?'

He smirks. 'Yep.'

Either side of the highway is a lush green. Farmhouses dot the countryside. It's a nice day. For a moment, I just look outwards. But then something inside me changes, like a switch being flicked. I'm tired of talking around things. I'm exhausted from avoiding the truth.

'I can't.'

'Can't what?' His eyes glance to mine.

'I can't have kids. Premature ovarian failure. Basically, it means I used up all of my eggs before I was twenty-five. A woman in her late forties has a better shot at getting knocked up than I do.'

'I'm so sorry, Iz.' He shakes his head, looking at the highway in front of him. 'I had no idea.'

I shrug. 'It's okay.'

For five minutes, no conversation passes between us. Turning to the window, I go back to the watching the scenery. There's a field of cows. A few sheep. It's not great land for growing food, but the livestock do well.

He doesn't push for anything else. I remember something I had always liked about him; he was easy to talk to. I could never trust my mother with a secret. By the time I got to high school, I'd learnt to hold back. Liam was the first person I could talk to. How had I forgotten that?

'We tried, Ben and me. It didn't happen. Sometimes it takes years to find out why someone can't conceive. Often they don't find why. It only took six weeks for me to get a diagnosis.'

He nods, listening.

'I had IVF. The first transfer worked, but I lost the pregnancy early on. After two more rounds, I gave up.'

Something about telling him made me feel free. I used to feel strong for keeping my secrets to myself. But some secrets have been keeping me.

After a minute, he speaks. 'There are other ways to have children in your life.'

The specialist had told me about other options. There was egg donation. There was adoption. Whenever I think about it, I get overwhelmed.

'Maybe one day. I'm not ready for that.'

Liam flicks on his indicator and leaves the highway. We are almost back to Cape Cross.

'You want me to take you home?' he asks.

'Yeah,' I nod.

21

ISOBEL

Liam wants to come inside, but I usher him away. He's already gone when I notice my front door is unlocked and open. Again. My heart flips in my chest. Has someone been inside? Is someone still in there?

Since I found my door open and a note on my bed, I've become hypervigilant. I've had a second deadlock installed as well as a door chain which secures from the inside. There are cameras I can check from my phone, sensor lights and a monitored alarm.

With my arm that isn't bandaged, I push the door open a few more inches. There's no one in sight.

'Hello?' I call.

At first, silence. Then I hear the clamour of someone moving around on the timber floors upstairs. I take a backwards step, off the concrete front porch and on to the garden bed. Someone is in there.

Liam is gone, his car already around the corner. Should I call him? He would only be a few streets away. In my handbag, I reach my hand in and feel the sleek plastic cover of my phone. I'm still walking backwards, heading to the street. Pressing my fingerprint on the screen, the phone unlocks.

Two weeks ago, I would have called the police. I don't trust them anymore. Liam can be here faster. He's the safer option. I dial his number and count the rings as I wait for him to answer.

'Isobel?'

It's not Liam, the voice isn't coming from my phone. Someone is calling me from inside the house. I let the phone drop to my side, still ringing.

'Isobel is that you?'

I look up and my mother is coming down the stairs, her pace slow and uneven. There is a slight hunch to her and a film of sweat on her face.

'Mum?'

'Isobel! I've been looking for you all morning? Where the hell have you been?'

'Why are you here, Mum? God, I was about to call the police.'

With a click on the red button I cut the call to Liam. When I get closer, I see she doesn't look good. There are dark circles under her eyes.

'Mum, what's going on? Come on, let's go upstairs.'

She turns and takes the stairs slowly, one at a time.

'Go sit down, Mum. I'll make you a tea.'

What is she doing here? I left a copy of the new key at their house. It was a backup, in case I got locked out or lost my bag somewhere. It wasn't an invitation to come in. Given both her and Dad hate coming here, I never thought I needed to state that explicitly.

Has she been in here before? If she wasn't already so agitated, I'd demand an answer.

Instead, I direct to her to the kitchen table and flick the kettle on. I pull out two cups from an overhead cupboard, and place a teabag in each while the water boils.

'What happened to your arm?' she says.

'I cut in on some glass. An accident. I needed a few stitches; I've been at the hospital.'

Twelve stitches, but I wasn't going to volunteer that.

'You went all the way to Waringal?' she raises her eyebrows.

I nod. 'I didn't want to spend half the day in a waiting room. It's easier to go to the hospital.'

'Why didn't you answer the phone?'

My bag is on the kitchen bench. I fish my phone out and look at the screen. Four missed calls from Mum. Two from Dad. And now one from Liam who has called me back already. 'Sorry, I leave it on silent a lot.'

'Well, don't.' The bluntness of her voice shocks me. 'Not at the moment. Not with everything that's going on.'

The kettle lets out a gurgle as it boils and flicks itself off. I pour hot water into the two cups, then take out the tea bags.

'That's not how you make tea, Isobel,' she says. 'You're meant to let the tea bag sit. You're not meant to move it like that.'

I ignore her. Dad's the only one who takes on board criticism like that. I place the tea in front of her and sit on the chair opposite here.

'What do you mean by everything that's going on?' I ask.

She looks in the cup. 'You forgot milk.'

'Mum, what do you mean? Is that why you are here? Has something happened to Dad?'

She shakes her head. 'Haven't you considered your own safety?'

'What?'

'Someone in this town was murdered. No one has any clue who did it. That means there's still a murderer at large.'

'Mum, whoever killed Veronica had a problem with her. It

was personal.' I take a sip of my tea. She's right, it's better with milk.

'What, and you don't think you've pissed people off? You're a divorce lawyer. There would be hundreds of people out there with a grudge against you.'

I roll my eyes. 'You watch too many legal dramas on television. Statistically, Veronica's killer was known to her. It could have been a lover. Maybe a client. Who knows?'

She shrugs and takes a sip of her tea.

'Is Dad alright?'

'He's fine.'

'And what about the police? Have they questioned him again?'

She shakes her head. 'No. Have they spoken to you?'

'Yes. But it's not related... I thought there was a break-in here. I think I left the door unlocked.' I grimaced. She was going to tell me off for that.

'When?'

'What?'

'When did you think someone broke in?'

'Um, Monday? Last week. It wasn't a break in though. I don't think I pulled the door shut properly.' There's no way I'm telling her about the note.

'Why did you think that?'

'The front door was unlocked… Mum, were you here then too?'

'No!' she says. She looks over to the kitchen.

'Why are you here, Mum?'

'You didn't answer the phone. Are you upset I came inside?'

'I'm not upset but you scared the shit out of me. I thought someone had broken in.'

'I was worried. I thought you might be here. I just… I've just been overreacting to things lately. It's not nice to have your husband be a murder suspect.'

'I don't think he's a murder suspect. I think he drives the wrong type of car.'

'So, is your arm alright?' She points at the bandage that stretches from my wrist to my elbow.

'It's fine, Mum. Just a silly accident.' She seems worried. More than she should be. I think about the brittle bone diagnosis and the conversation with the doctor and wonder again why she would keep it from me. There is enough drama at the moment. I decide it's going to be easier if I just go get tested and don't say anything.

'Where's the glass? You want some help cleaning up?' She stands, picks up her empty cup and places it on the bench next to the sink.

'Nope. It was somewhere else. I was with a friend.' I stand up as well.

'Which friend?'

'What's with the inquisition today, Mum?'

'Inquisition?'

'You're asking a lot of questions.'

She puts her hands on the table. 'I just want to know you're alright. I worry about you.'

'Everything's fine, Mum. Just… next time you want to come inside let me know first.'

'Answer your phone next time and I will.'

It's not long before she leaves, proving the fact that both her and Dad hate being inside this house. My absence this morning must have really rocked her. I feel a little guilty and then try and shake it off. I'm not responsible for other people's emotions.

Something is up. It could be stress over Dad, but this isn't just stress. She's acting irrationally.

With a sigh, I turn away from the window. I need to go figure out a way to shower with this bandage on my arm. Before I can make my way to the bathroom, something in the study catches my eye. The filing cabinet drawer is wide open again.

22

MAYA

Isobel Franco is not flexible. I mean that literally. When I invited her to yoga she hesitated before she agreed, maybe I should have read into that a little more. We arrive a minute before class starts and take the last available spots.

Isobel is on the yoga mat in front of me. She's wearing a pair of black shorts and a Lululemon halter top. If I didn't already know she was a runner, I would be able to tell from the muscle definition on her legs. And the fact that her arms aren't strong enough to hold her in down dog for more than thirty seconds.

The yoga studio is white and sparse in a way that's meant to be relaxing. I suppose simple can be relaxing. Organisation is what relaxes me. Knowing where everything is. Knowing what's going to happen. I like to keep the chaos at bay.

This is my usual class I take every week. Of course, I've been absent the last two weeks. Lucy suggested I start coming again, even if I didn't feel like it.

The other reason I'm here is that I lied to David yesterday. It didn't turn out well, he saw right through it. Now I feel like I'm trying to back up my lie, even though it's too late. I figured I might as well rope Isobel into coming. If nothing else, I'll have an alibi.

Yoga is not her thing. She looks lost and I think she's a stranger to stretching. The instructor, with a perfect messy bun and the skin of someone who lives on air and avocados, orders us in to a twist. Isobel turns around and faces the back of the room. I smile, catching her gaze. Her weak smile back looks more like a cry for help.

'Sorry,' I mouth. She shrugs and grits her teeth.

I've seen her running out on the cliff road a few times, so I know she's fit. It's hard to miss her in the expensive running gear. The woman has a lot of pricey stuff for someone that has no apparent interest in money or brand names. Maybe she doesn't look at the price tags. Maybe she walks into a shop and buys whatever thing she likes most.

Isobel fumbles her way through the forty-minute class. The moment it's over, she leaves for the change room stuffing her feet into her shoes and putting her oversized hoodie back on. I'm close behind her, grabbing my canvas gym bag out of a locker on the way out.

'That was awful,' she says as soon as the glass door to the studio closes behind us. It's ten o'clock on a Saturday morning. It's not hot yet, but the sharp bite of the sun tells me the afternoon will warm up.

'I'm sorry,' I say. 'I thought you might like it.'

'No, I'm glad I did it. All I do is run. I can't even touch my toes, I'm so inflexible. Part of the reason I decided to come back here was to try and get a bit more work-life balance. Try and focus on health.'

'How's that working out?' I raise an eyebrow.

'All life, no work,' she says with a smile.

From the road I can make out the blue sea blending with the horizon. This is my favourite time of year. Late Spring, almost summer. Warm enough to be outside, not so hot that you sweat twenty-three hours a day.

'It's been a strange time.' She continues. 'My boyfriend from Melbourne was meant to move here with me. He changed his mind at the last minute.'

'Oh. Sorry. I heard something like that.'

She nods. 'It's fine.'

'Were you together long?'

'A few years. Anyway, then all this other stuff happened. I've been worried about my Dad.'

I nod. 'It feels like that was just a mistake. I mean, the police haven't questioned him again.'

'Not as far as I know,' she says. 'He's not a talker. He keeps a lot to himself.'

There's a large, square bandage on the underside of Isobel's arm. 'What did you do there?'

'It's okay now. It got cut on some glass and needed a couple of stitches. I get them out on Tuesday.'

'No wonder you were struggling in that class,' I grin.

She shakes her head. 'It doesn't hurt, it's just uncomfortable. I don't think I can really blame a cut on my arm for my lack of core strength.'

I laugh. 'Have you got time for coffee?'

Isobel nods. 'Yeah, sure.'

The shops are closer to the water and the small shady inlet of Safety Beach. It's the only place you can swim in Cape Cross. Well, if you don't want to die that is. The surfers tend to get in the water wherever the waves are, rips be damned. We walk down the hill towards the shore, the coffee shop being the last shop on the corner before the road ends and turns to foreshore.

An open window with a wide sill allows you to order a take-away without going inside the shop.

'What do you have?' I ask Isobel.

'Long black.'

I might have guessed it. Isobel was no nonsense. She was the same in high school. I get the sense things are black and white for her. Every break up, setback and bad grade I'd ever had would plague me for months afterwards. Not Isobel. She shrugged it off like nothing happened. She moved on. She got things done.

Veronica was a different person again. She didn't worry about black and white, she pushed until the world was whatever colour she wanted. I'd heard her on the phone with clients, talking them around and around until they agreed to an offer. She had a gift. It wasn't always ethical, but it was something.

I order for us both.

'Want to walk along the pier?' asks Isobel.

'Sure.'

The small wooden pier hadn't been used by boats for years. Kids liked to jump off it in summer, and occasionally someone would fish off the end. A proper boat ramp was installed a few kilometres away.

'I can't imagine there are a lot of jobs for lawyers out here.' I take a sip of my coffee.

'There's a few jobs in Waringal. When I first planned the move, I wanted to open my own practice. I even looked at a few shops.' Her tone tells me she had changed her mind.

'But?'

'Once I got here... I don't know. It's like I lost momentum.' She sighs a little, as if she is disappointed.

'Like you said, a lot of stuff has happened. I'm sure you'll work it out.'

We reach the end of the pavement, and walk across the warm sand towards the pier.

'I was talking to Liam Goddard the other day.' Isobel says. 'You know, he was top of our class. He could have been a doctor and he chucked it in to manage a pub. He has a degree in biomedical science.'

'Oh yeah. He was smart in high school.'

I keep my voice cool, but I was dying to ask where she saw him. They had a history. I wouldn't be surprised if they were back on again. But I held my tongue. Isobel could tell me if she wanted to. Our rekindled friendship was young, and I didn't want to speak out of turn.

'Do you guys see each other much?' Okay, so I couldn't help it.

'A few times. Not on purpose, actually.' She looks out over the water. It was unusually calm today. 'He was saying, we do all these things because we think we should. We become doctors, because they're more valuable than bartenders. But, what's really better? You know, I don't make that much money. Not considering the years of university and the ridiculous hours I'm expected to commit.'

'I get your point. David did a trade and he pulls six figures.'

'Well, he's making more than me. I went to university for five years.'

I laugh. 'He was working full time at seventeen. You must like it though. There must be something about it or you wouldn't be doing it.'

'There are good bits. But if I had my time again, I wouldn't repeat myself.'

I turned to her, surprised. 'Really?'

Isobel nods.

'What would you do?'

'I don't know. In fact, I never gave it a lot of thought. Work's work and all that. But Liam's got me thinking.'

'What's his deal, anyway? He doesn't want to be a doctor?' I wonder if there is another reason he gave it up.

'He was a researcher. He said he likes his life better now. He gets to surf.' she shrugs.

'Bloody surfers.'

Isobel laughs. 'Doesn't David surf?'

'Exactly. Nothing worse than finally having him home for a day and he buggers off down the beach for three hours.'

'He works long hours?' she asks.

I nod and hesitate before I speak again. 'Yeah. He has to.'

'Tell him to surf less. He could spend more time with you all.'

I laugh out loud at that.

'What's funny?' Her brows furrow with concern and I think I've given too much away.

I smile, downplaying my reaction. 'He's very rigid. When things don't happen the way he wants them too he gets… a bit withdrawn.'

'Withdrawn,' she repeats. 'Silent treatment?'

I shrug. Withdrawn is not the right word. He does go silent, but he is simmering. By the time that happens, it's too late to prevent the explosion that's coming.

'That's a hard one,' offers Isobel. 'There's always difficult things that you have to talk about. If you can't for risk of being ostracised… well, that's a difficult relationship to be in.'

I nod, even though her advice is off the mark. How could it be right when I haven't told her the truth? Just like I'm not telling her the whole truth, there's a lot I don't tell David as well. I wonder just how much energy I spend avoiding conflict.

Something vibrates inside Isobel's bag. She pulls out her phone. Looking at the screen she screws her face up, and declines the call.

'Who is it?' I ask.

'I don't know the number. Probably market research. I get a lot of stuff like that lately.'

'I hate unknown callers.'

We walk back to the sand and then make our way up the hill towards where we had both parked our cars that morning. Isobel's phone makes a low beep. She looks at the screen again, biting her lip.

'Everything okay?' I ask.

'Edmund Keane just left me a message.' Isobel doesn't look up; her eyes are fixed on her phone.

'Who's Edmund Keane?' I ask. The name is familiar but I can't place it.

'He's a lawyer,' Isobel answers.

'Oh yeah. He was at the funeral. What does he want?'

'I have no idea. I've never spoken a word to him.'

'It's probably nothing. He could have called the wrong person.'

Isobel shakes her head. She looks thoroughly spooked.

23

ISOBEL

The first time I call, the receptionist tells me I'll need to wait six weeks to see a genetic counsellor. A day later, a different person calls back and says there's been a cancellation that afternoon if I want it.

Less than a week after I had my arm stitched up at the hospital, I am back in Waringal again. This time I am waiting in the specialist rooms, opposite the hospital.

Liam called me last night, and I almost told him what was going on. For some reason, he's the only person I trust right now. Is it because we have history? Could it be that easy to fall back into an old pattern?

I didn't talk about it. We didn't talk about Max Hayes either. Or Veronica. Instead we talked about things that happened in high school, about missing Melbourne coffee and how house prices are crazy right now. The dark stuff stayed underneath the surface.

So now I am sitting in a waiting room alone, wondering if I have a genetic disease that my mother has kept hidden from me.

The doctor is running late, I wait a full twenty minutes before he calls me in. He has deep horizontal lines across his forehead and thin, wavy hair.

'So, Brittle Bone in the family,' he says as I take the tub chair opposite him. There is a heavy timber desk between the two of us. His eyes are on a printed report in front of him, not on me.

'Your mother was diagnosed two years back.' He squints when he speaks and I wonder if the poor guy needs glasses.

'Yes.'

'You didn't want to find out before now?'

I nod and opened my mouth to speak, but he interrupts me.

'Sorry,' he says. 'The counsellor probably went through that with you. I don't want to bore you.'

I close my mouth. I haven't seen a counsellor. Have I skipped a step in the process? There's no chance to say anything before he continues. It could be a good thing, this way I'll find out the truth faster.

'She has type one. Well, if you had to choose, that would be the pick.' He's reading the report again.

Why were doctors so weird and impersonal? Maybe that was why Liam quit. The doctor squints again.

'How are your teeth?'

'Fine.'

'No fillings, pain?'

'No, all normal.' I haven't seen a dentist in four years, but I assume my teeth are fine.

'Any joint pain?'

'Nope.'

'And did you break a bone as a child?'

'I broke my arm when I was twelve.'

He nods, 'Respiratory issues, heart problems? Nothing out of the ordinary at all?'

'No. I'm normal. Totally normal.'

'Not likely,' he said. 'Everyone has something wrong with them.'

I go to answer but I'm not really sure what to say to him. He's right. Everyone does have something wrong with them. Then it occurs to me what it is and I can't believe it's slipped my mind.

'Oh. Premature ovarian failure. I was diagnosed a few years back.' I surprise myself with how even my voice stays.

He presses his lips together. 'Any kids?'

I shake my head. 'No.'

'And you're…' he looks at the report again. 'Thirty-two.'

He nods but doesn't speak for a minute. 'It's very unlikely you carry the gene. If you did, we'd be seeing signs by now, however small. You'll want to know though, especially when you get to menopause. The test is covered by Medicare, so you won't be out of pocket.'

'Great. I'd rather know.'

That would be a double whammy. You've run out of eggs, your body doesn't make collagen and now all your bones are going to break.

'Easy,' he says. He glances up from his paperwork, this time not squinting.

'You remind me of your mother.' He grins, breaking his flat expression. 'She always asks me to tell it like it is. You've got her hair too. With a bit of luck, you missed out on some of the other genes. I've been seeing Jennifer since her diagnosis. I've never had a patient that asks so many questions.'

I nod. 'That sounds like Mum.'

'Okay,' he says. 'We will take some blood today and we'll schedule a results appointment in six weeks.'

He goes to stand up but then he stops.

'Do you know your blood type?'

'Sure, it's O-negative. I used to donate.' The Red Cross had a permanent station set up near my old office in Melbourne.

'Yeah...' his voice trails off. 'It says that here too.' Something like concern flashes across his face.

'What's wrong?'

'Nothing. Bear with me. I've got to check something.'

The doctor leaves the consult room, closing the door behind him. I stay in the chair, waiting. Outside, I could hear a hum of voices from the waiting room and the faint crackle of a radio.

When he comes back, there is a manilla folder in his hand. A printed sticky label on the tab had a familiar name.

Jennifer Franco.

It's my mother's file. He opens it on the desk, flicks through a few pages and then shakes his head. When he looks up at me, his brow is furrowed and there is something in his eyes I don't recognise. He looks like he is about to give me bad news. He takes a deep breath, but then his face softens.

'Right. Well, let's organise this blood test. I might get my nurse to come give me a hand, she's far less likely to leave you with a nasty bruise.'

He leaves the room again. Whatever he was about to tell me, he changed his mind. Was it something to do with me or my mother? It was my O-negative blood that had upset him. What was so terrible about that? Did it mean I had a higher chance of having Brittle Bone disease?

The file is still on his desk, open. Leaning over, I reach for it, spinning it around so I can read the page the doctor has left open. It's my mother's intake form. Her full name is listed, her date of birth, and details like height and weight. I scan it with my eyes, looking for a clue. I see her blood type: A-positive.

Why had he wanted to check this file? I can't work out what he was looking for. I pull my phone from my handbag and take photos of the first few pages.

A-positive. And me, O-negative.

What does that mean? I don't know anything about blood types. I don't even know if that was the detail he had fixated on. Before I can think it through any more, a middle-aged woman with short black hair comes in. The doctor is close behind her.

'We'll get these tests organised pronto and then move forward,' he says. His tone is strained.

'Stay in that chair, honey,' says the nurse in a warm voice. She bends over and clips a brightly coloured tourniquet around my forearm. My eyes fix on the roof while she draws four vials of blood.

'That's a lot,' I comment.

'We send everything to two labs in case of a false result,' says the doctor. 'Mistakes are very rare but they happen.'

They finish up, I hand over my Medicare card at reception and then I walk back out to my car. O-negative. Was that recessive? I sit for a minute, churning it over in my head before I turn on the engine.

There is something going on. Recessive genes and dominant genes. A high school biology memory comes floating back. I need help from someone who knows something about genetics.

As soon as my car's Bluetooth picks up my phone, I dial Liam.

'Hello?' He answers. He sounds surprised.

'Liam?'

'Yeah?'

'I've got a really important question. Can a parent with A-positive blood type have a child that is O-negative?'

24

ISOBEL

'It's a complicated question.'

I'm sitting on the same barstool as the last time I was at the pub. Again, Liam is opposite me on the other side of the timber bar. However, this time the place is empty. It's 2pm in the afternoon and the pub doesn't open until five. We are the only people here.

'But first of all, I think you need a drink.' says Liam, looking me over as he speaks. That seems to be his answer for a lot of things.

'You've got a medical degree,' I say. 'Look at these reports. My mother is hiding something from me.' I hold up my phone showing the photos of the documents I photographed in the doctor's office.

'I don't have a medical degree. It's biomedical science. That's like me calling you an accountant.'

'Not really,' I answer. 'I can't do your taxes, but I reckon you can help me figure this out.'

Liam pours two beers from the tap and places them in front of me. He jumps over the bar and then takes the barstool next to mine.

'So, I think you've got to tell me the whole story. From the beginning,' he says.

When I'd called him from the car, he had avoided answering my questions. Instead, he kept talking in a steady voice, telling me to drive to the pub. I'd come straight here from Waringal.

'I don't think Mum is my mum,' I say. The look on his face tells me that he isn't following my logic. 'I saw some stuff at an appointment today. I took photos.'

Liam takes my phone from my hands, flicking through the photos of the medical documents that I had snapped in the specialist's office.

'Well, first of all, this is a massive privacy violation,' he says, his eyes still fixed to the screen.

'The doctor left it there to be violated,' I counter.

'It could have been an accident.' He doesn't meet my eyes, instead uses his thumb and forefinger to zoom in on a photo. 'I'm not totally comfortable with this.'

'Why? You don't even work as a doctor anymore.'

'I was never a doctor. You know that.' This time he does look at me, his eyes narrowed. 'I still have an ethical responsibility.'

'Says the man who broke into a hospital last week.'

Again, he is real queasy when it comes to anything illegal. He was the same about the hospital. Has he been in trouble before, or is he taking steps to avoid it in the future?

'As did you,' he says. What does that mean? He'll tell on me if I tell on him? It doesn't matter either way. I need his help right now, the rest I can worry about another day.

'There's a lot at stake here. I really need your help,' I say.

'Okay,' He sighs. My hand is resting on the bar. He gently places his own on top. I flinch a little but I don't move away. 'I never had anything to do with this, if anyone ever asks.'

I nod.

'The thing is, Mum can't keep a secret. Not if she tried. I found out that I could have Brittle Bone disease, it's genetic apparently. But she's never told me that or said I should get tested.'

He shrugs. 'Sometimes people can surprise you with what are hiding.'

'What if she didn't tell me because I didn't need to know? If I'm not her biological child, there's no risk. And maybe telling me would reveal something else.'

'That you have different parents?'

I nod. 'If that's true, I need to know.'

He thinks about it, leaning back a little. 'So, you know that you carry two genes for blood type?'

'Kind of. I think we did it in high school, right?'

'You have two genes. O is a recessive blood type. To have O blood, both of the genes you are carrying have to be type O.'

'So, she can't be my mother? Not if she has A type blood?'

He shook his head. 'Not necessarily. It's more complicated than that. She could have AO blood. So her type would be A, but she could pass on the O gene to you.'

'Right. So, all of this could mean nothing? I'm drawing massive paranoid conclusions?'

Did I imagine the look on the doctor's face earlier today? Perhaps everything that is happening has put my brain on overdrive.

'I don't know, Iz. Maybe.' He places my phone down on the timber counter. 'You need to know your Dad's blood type. Is there any way you could find out?'

I drum my fingers on the bar. 'He came into the city one day. I used to donate blood, there was a centre close to work. One day, he was in Melbourne. He came and had lunch with me. I mentioned I was donating afterwards and he came with me.'

'Right, so you know from then?'

'I'm not totally sure. But I remember him making a joke

about it. That his blood couldn't make up its mind, he had two types.'

'Two types. Do you remember the type?'

'I want to say AB. He said it was rare.'

'AB negative is the rarest blood type.'

I nod. 'So, there's no way I could have O blood. I'm impossible.'

'There's a lot of factors that you're unsure about. The best thing to do is sit down with them and talk. There could be an explanation for all of this.'

'Like what? I was adopted?'

'I don't know.' He picks up his glass, taking a long sip. 'Maybe you were adopted and they never wanted to tell you. Maybe you have different Dad and your Mum didn't want anyone to know. Or maybe she didn't realise until later.'

I shake my head. 'She's keeping something from me. The other day when you dropped me off, the front door to my house was wide open. I was about to call the police when I realised it was her. She let her herself inside. She was sitting at the kitchen table.'

'Your Mum came to visit you. What's wrong with that?'

'Well, she never visits me, I visit her. I gave her a key for emergencies. It's totally out of character for her to use it. And when she left, my filing cabinet was wide open.'

He shrugs. 'Did you leave it open? What's in the cabinet anyway?'

'The usual stuff. Tax returns. Medical records.'

Liam tilts his head in thought. 'What would she even be looking for?'

'I don't know. That's what I'm trying to work out. What if one of them isn't my parent? Or both of them. Maybe she was looking for something medical.'

Liam lets out a huff of air. 'Iz, I get you're looking for an explanation. But this is getting farfetched. You look like your Mum. Whenever I see your Dad I do a double-take, you're the only two people in the world with those pale green eyes. I'd be incredibly shocked if they weren't your parents. You could have misremembered the conversation with your father. There could be a mistake with your own blood type. Your parents love you. They wouldn't do anything to harm you.'

'Then why? Why are all of these strange, terrible things happening to me? I stumble over a dead body while I go running. Someone's been creeping in my house. Then everyone I know is hauled into a police station over a murder.'

'I think it's unfortunate. I think this is a small town and you were in the wrong place at the wrong time. The rest of it… everyone knows that Veronica and I dated and it didn't always go smoothly. Maya was her friend. And your Dad just drove the wrong kind of car.'

'Someone was following me in a car. It felt like a warning.'

I bite my bottom lip. With my left hand, I move the glass on the bar around in a semi-circle. I haven't drunk any of it.

'Maybe you need to give yourself a break. Sometimes terrible things happen. It can be hard to accept. It's awful that someone hurt Veronica. I can't stop thinking about it. But the police are working on it. That's what they do. And I'll bet the reason that the investigation has gone quiet is because they know who did it. They will be getting their case together. It can take time; they'll want to have their evidence straight. You should let them do their job.'

I nod.

'Why don't you leave it all alone for a while?' he says. 'Stop worrying about blood types. And definitely stop thinking about Veronica Hayes.'

I understand his argument but I don't know if I can let things go.

'What are you doing this week?' His hand is still on mine. It sounds like he wants to change the subject.

'This week? I don't know,' I answer.

'Do you want to do something?'

'What? Like break into a hospital together?'

'I was thinking something less illegal. Like Thai food and Netflix.'

I look out of the window towards the car park. His question has caught me off guard.

'Maybe we should wait for things to be normal before we act normal,' I answer.

His face falls. I regret the words as soon as they come out of my mouth. The only reason I'm turning him down is because I feel guilty. But he wasn't dating Veronica, they weren't even speaking. And things are well and truly over between Ben and me. There isn't a real reason to say no.

I put my hand on his arm. 'You know what? Things are never normal. What night is good for you?'

Liam smiles. He opens his mouth to answer but my phone rings. The ringer is on all the time now after the episode with Mum.

'Sorry,' I apologise, reaching for the phone. When I see the caller, I sigh.

'Who is it?' Liam leans forward in his barstool.

'Edmund Keane. He's called a few times. He's a lawyer.'

He narrows his eyes. 'Yeah, I know him.'

'He keeps calling. Normally, I would have returned the call but… things keep getting in the way.'

'Don't mind me if you want to grab it,' he offers.

'No.' I reject the call and put the phone on the bar beside me. I give Liam my attention again. But there is concern on his face now. 'What's wrong?'

'What does he want from you?'

'He knows I looked at office space. He just wants to suss out what I'm doing. He left a voicemail about a meeting.'

'Are you sure that's why?'

'No. I'm just guessing. I don't think he and my grandfather were on good terms. He probably doesn't want me working around here.' I shrug.

'Maybe it's something else. Edmund Keane owns the old hospital site. If Veronica was trying to sell it, he would be the person she was making a deal with.'

25

MAYA

A white truck lets out a long beep as it reverses up Dad's short driveway. One tanned arm out of the window, the driver gives a brief wave at my father. He waves back from the porch, standing crooked with one hand on his hip and the other on his oxygen tank. He looks concerned but it could be the sun in his eyes.

It takes two men to bring the hospital bed into the house. I leave them to assemble it; I'll probably just get in the way. Dad's old bed is already out on the back veranda. I dismantled it earlier this morning and dragged it out there on my own.

Dad walks back inside, letting out a sigh when he stops beside me. What does it feel like to look at a bed in a room and know that you will die there? I suppose the alternative is worse; waiting to spend your last days in a soulless hospital room.

The driver brings in a large cardboard box. It must be the

handrails and the rest of the order. 'Where's this one going then?' He asks, directing the question at both of us.

'In here is fine,' I answer. I'll go through it once the bed is done. The driver nods and puts the box down on the floor.

Dad turns his head towards me. 'Is David coming over to put the rails up?'

I shake my head. 'He has work.' In truth, I didn't mention anything about the delivery today to David. Instead, I searched how to put the rails up on YouTube. There's a cordless drill in the back of my car.

David has said less than ten words to me since we argued in the kitchen. He offers no explanations of what happened the night Veronica disappeared. I don't ask him for them. We move around the house from room to room, circling each other, listening but never talking. It feels like a game of chess where we move our pawns backward and forwards, never making a real move.

It's a game I've played too long. The night he grabbed my arm should have been the end of our relationship. The purple imprint of his fingers took days to fade. David was drunk. So was I. It was a perfect storm, one I have worked hard to make sure will never come together again.

I tread carefully around him. I do everything exactly the way he likes. The threat lies underneath everything, that if I don't, I'll see the same dark side of him.

I think about what Isobel said: a relationship where you can't communicate is impossible. I have not been honest for years. It's how I keep our lives clean of conflict. How can you be loved by someone who you can't be honest with? Without truth, they don't really see you. You can't be loved if you can't be seen.

Dad is out the front, waving off the delivery truck. I'm in the kitchen, opening and closing drawers, looking for something to open the last box with. There's no scissors, the best I can come up with is an old steak knife.

I take it back to the lounge where Dad has sat in one of the old armchairs, his body sunken and his shoulders hunched. He has his oxygen mask clamped to his face.

'You okay?'

He nods. 'I'm fine, love.'

Holding the box steady with one hand, I saw through the masking tape and then yank the edges open. I lay the handrails on the coffee table. On the website they looked white. In reality, they're closer to cream.

'Isn't it right?' Dad has read the expression on my face.

'The colour is different,' I say.

He shrugs. 'No matter. Will David have time on the weekend?'

'I thought I'd give it a shot,' I answer. 'That way it's all done for you.' I try to smile as I speak.

He grimaces. 'I can wait until Saturday. It's no problem.'

Nothing is going to change between David and I before then. The problem is, I don't really want to speak to him. I don't want him to help.

'What's wrong?' Dad asks.

'Nothing.'

'There is something. I can always tell.'

'It's David.' I let out a rush of air I didn't know I was holding in. 'Things are tough at the moment.'

'Oh. A rough patch, eh?'

'Something like that.' I put the box to one side and sit beside him.

'Everyone has them, darling. It'll pass.' He pats the back of my hand with his own.

'I'm not waiting for it to pass, Dad. I don't want to be with him.' The words shock me as I say them. I didn't know they were coming.

'Oh. Oh, Maya. David's a good man. I've known him since he was a boy. Maybe the two of you could go talk to someone? A counsellor?'

I shake my head. 'No. He's good a lot of the time. But other times are… awful.'

I don't have the heart to tell him about the time he grabbed me or about how I have always felt some level of fear around him ever since. Dad waits for me to say more.

'He gets drunk. Sometimes he breaks things. Other times he just yells.'

'Breaks things? What kind of things? When did this start happening?' His eyes widen.

'A few years ago now. It's not all the time. The first time he was drunk. The other times we were fighting. He smashed a plate on the floor once. Another time he threw Jacob's Nintendo at a window.'

Dad is silent for a full minute. 'Have you spoken to him about it?'

'I can't. I can't talk to him about anything. I'm always afraid he'll blow up over something.'

'You'll have to have a conversation with him. Even if you want to separate, you'll have to tell him.'

'You're right,' I say, and he is. But even contemplating having that conversation fills my body up with anxiety. There's no way I can actually do it. How would he react? Stone cold silence or white-hot rage?

'Are you safe?' asks Dad.

'Yes,' I answer. I think I am.

We both are silent now, looking straight ahead at the wall on the opposite side of the room. I don't know how much time passes. There is a kind of sadness in the air, but I also feel relief. I've finally said the words out loud.

'You know, you can come here. Any time you want. You

don't need to let me know. You can show up on my doorstep and time, day or night. There's a spare room here, two if you count your mother's sewing room. We could fix that up nice for the boys.'

'Thanks, Dad.' It's a generous offer. Maybe it could work. 'I'll keep it in mind.'

'Right then. I'll go put the kettle on.'

26

ISOBEL

As much as I want to, I don't call Edmund Keane back straight away. Instead, I say goodbye to Liam and drive myself home. Standing in my kitchen, I wonder what his relationship was to Veronica. And why he is interested in me. As I lean against the bench, I dial the number the lawyer left and wait for him to pick up.

I scold myself for not paying attention to his phone calls earlier. The link I have been looking for could be close.

'Good afternoon. Edmund Keane speaking.'

'Mr Keane. It's Isobel Franco speaking. I missed your call.'

There's a pause before he answers. 'Miss Franco,' he says, his tone cool. 'Finally, we speak.'

'I'm sorry. I did get your message. It's been a hectic time.'

'I understand. When I saw you the other week I almost came and spoke to you then. Of course, it was the wrong place.' He is talking about the funeral. It wasn't my imagination; he was looking at me that day.

My gut wants me to ask him about the old hospital site straight away. Did he know Veronica? Was she trying to do a deal with him or someone else?

'I've been wanting to set a meeting with you. It's well overdue,' he says.

'Okay.' That doesn't give away much. 'Is this something we can speak about over the phone?'

'No.' His answer is firm. 'It's of a personal nature so I think best dealt with in person. Anyhow, my instructions are to meet with you.'

'Instructions? From who?'

'Like I said, it's not the kind of thing we should discuss over the phone.'

'Right.' I wasn't going to get anywhere with a phone call. 'When are you thinking?'

'How about tomorrow, late in the day. Say six pm?'

'Okay.' I hesitate. That is late in the day, almost like he doesn't want anyone to be around. 'Is this about Veronica Hayes?'

Silence. I wait for him to speak first. I count to ten but he still hasn't said anything.

'It's best I see you in person,' he says finally. 'I can fill you in on everything then, Miss Franco.'

Edmund Keane hangs up before I can ask another question. Nothing new has been revealed, I'm going to have to meet him in person.

Veronica had been angry that my grandfather did a deal behind her back once. Had Edmund Keane done the same thing? Could she have confronted him?

Still, none of that could explain why he wanted to speak to me now. What could I have to do with any of it?

Frustration was becoming a familiar feeling. Like most people, I like closure. When a television series ends with a cliffhanger, I can't stand it. Let alone something that happens in real life.

Maybe Google is my friend. I'd spent a lot of time searching Veronica, but not Edmund Keane. I walk towards my study. Opening my laptop, I click on the internet browser. I type both their names into the search bar.

'Edmund Keane, Veronica Hayes'

All of the results are recent news articles about Veronica. There is nothing there to link the two of them together. I try searching for Edmund Keane without Veronica's name.

The first page is his professional website and brief mentions of his work in the media. On the second page, I find an application to the local council to extend his house and a picture of him and his wife playing tennis at the local club. They're both smiling and wearing white polo shirts and those sweat bands around their wrists that were big in the eighties.

Since he's a lawyer, I search through the court records. I don't expect him to have any kind of criminal past, or he wouldn't be working. He's a country lawyer, I figure a lot of his clients are fighting over fence lines or updating their wills. But then I find something interesting.

There's an order placed by a court. It's something to do with a superannuation company he acts as trustee for. That's not unusual, it's probably a client. Often people have accountants set up these kinds of structures, but sometimes lawyers do it as well. It's the mailing address that gets my attention. It's a very familiar post office box. I've seen it on my grandfather's documents before.

I type out the full address into Google. That's where I find it. There's dozens of companies set up, using that address. And it looks like money has moved through all of them. One of them stands out.

The V and M Hayes Family Trust.

Veronica and Max Hayes. It's unusual for a single person to set up a family trust. There's no real benefit unless you're trying to minimise tax. Unless Veronica made a lot more money than she let on, or had received some kind of massive payday, there was no need for it.

What was she hiding?

I sigh out loud. I feel like all the pieces of a puzzle are in front of me, but I have no way to put them together.

27

MAYA

I don't want to go home.

David has a day off, he's there. He'll be waiting. This morning I said the four words I've been dreading.

'We need to talk.'

I didn't mean to say them. My timing was terrible. They fell out of my mouth without me thinking. As if the power to stop myself had been taken away. David didn't flinch, he kept packing the boys' lunches. He couldn't have thought I meant about educational options or paint colours or holidays. I stood on the other side of the kitchen bench, not moving, waiting for him to look up. When he finally did, he saw my face.

His eyes widened and he straightened his back. The knife he was spreading jam with was placed down on the bench. He waited for me to speak.

'Later. After the school run,' I said, backtracking.

'All right,' he agreed. 'I'll see you when you get back.'

His voice was flat and I wondered if he already knew what I was going to tell him. Maybe this is not the right thing.

I dropped the boys off out the front of their school. I used to walk in with them. They like it better now if I stop at the gate and let them squeeze out the back door all on their own, even though their backpacks are almost as big as they are. I wait a minute, watching them run towards their classroom.

I don't want to go home.

Now I am in the supermarket, walking up and down the aisles, putting things I don't need into my trolley. The cupboards are already full at home.

I blurted out those words and now I've started something I can't stop. A runaway train. An avalanche. When I tell David the truth, I'm going to have to tell him all of it. Which means everything about Veronica. Why did I do it?

Because you can't live like this. A voice in my own head answers my question.

There it is. That force in my unconscious that makes me act. We think we're in control of our lives. We think we control who we love and who we spend our time with. I'm not sure that's the case.

There are truths about ourselves that we can't escape. We can avoid them, living our lives around them. But they still exist.

There are pieces of myself that I'll never be free of. They wait on the periphery, like a constant anxiety. They eat away at everything. Given enough time, ignored for long enough, they'll cause the other parts of your life to collapse.

As long as I live in a house with a man I don't love, those feelings will be there. The anxiety will eat away at me like soda on rotten teeth. I deserve to be loved. So did Veronica.

David constantly puts me on edge, I'm always trying to do the right thing, trying to earn points in a game I don't understand. Until I become a version of myself I don't recognise. David was the yin to Veronica's yang. She took me as I was and never asked me to be anyone else. From the day I met her in mothers' group she was my closest confidante. She was my safe harbour. All those things David never gave me, she did. He knew that before I did.

If I had found this courage sooner, Veronica would still be alive. The first thought I had when I heard her body was found on the beach was that I could have prevented it.

'Maya?' A voice pulls me from my own thoughts.

I look up and see Liam Goddard standing next to me, putting apples in a string bag.

'Hi, Liam. Sorry, I was in my own world.' I smile, as if nothing is wrong.

'Yeah, I could tell. How are you doing?' His brow furrows as he asks, as if he expects me to answer in the negative.

'Fine. Just fine. Trying to get back to normal.'

He gives a weak smile. 'Isobel said the same thing to me the other day.'

I nod. To be honest, I haven't had a lot to do with Liam since high school. Everything I know about him came through Veronica. She never told me Liam was Max's father. There's a good chance there are other things she never told me. I wonder if he misses her. I wonder if he feels guilty like I do.

'I've got to ask you something.' He puts the bag of apples in his trolley behind him and steps closer. 'If it's okay.'

There's apples in my own cart but I don't remember putting them there. 'Sure.'

'Have you seen Max? Or Veronica's parents?' His face looks hopeful.

'I've seen Heather. Max was back at school this week.'

He nods. 'How is she?'

'Not good.' I don't think any of us are good.

'Do you think… would you talk to her for me? About Max? I don't think I'm on the birth certificate.'

'He's yours though Liam, isn't he?'

'She told me that, when he was born. We weren't really together. It was always off and on between us. I tried. I really stuffed things up with her though. I let her down.'

'You did?' Veronica never told me why things didn't work with them.

He nods. 'It was a dumb thing. A really dumb thing. I lost some money. Some of it was Veronica's. I thought I could pay it back, but I couldn't. If that costs me Max…'

'You broke up over money?' It was also the thing that came between me and her.

'I guess it was a part of what ended us,' Liam confirms.

Veronica did love money. Money for the sake of money. She had goals she was always chasing. Every day she had to speak with a certain amount of clients. That would lead to a certain amount of property listings. In turn, that gave her a level of commission. When I asked what she planned to do with all the money she looked lost. She never knew what she was going to do with the money, just that she wanted all of it. She certainly would not have liked someone losing her money.

I think of the day before she died, when we took the boys to the playground by the beach. I watched their heads bob around as they weaved around the playground equipment.

'You can't stay with him,' said Veronica.

'I don't have a choice.' She knew about David. Even if I wanted to, I could never keep a secret from her.

'Move in with me. We'll be fine. Like our own little family.' She linked her arm through mine and the red waves of her hair spilled over my chest. I let myself indulge in the thought for a moment. It could work. We understood each other. We parented in similar ways. And what was wrong with two mothers sharing a house? There was no other person that I'd rather spend my time with than her.

'I could live with you?'

'Of course you could. Pack a bag. Don't tell David. We'll work it out as we go.'

And there would be a lot to work out. Would I have to share custody? How would we all fit in Veronica's tiny house. And what about my Dad?

'I can't.'

'Are you afraid of David?'

'No. It's my Dad. He needs me.'

'He'll be okay. I know he's sick. But he'll want you to be happy.'

'It's not what he thinks that I'm worried about. I don't have a job, Veronica. I can't afford his medical bills on my own.'

She bit her lip, taking a moment before she spoke. 'I can. I'll help you.'

But I knew that she couldn't. She had a mortgage and a car loan plus the fees at the school. She made good money but it wouldn't carry all of us. I would never burden her like that. 'You have to look after yourself and Max.'

She shook her head. 'I know. You've told me before. Something I've been working on is about to pay off. It's going to be enough to look after your Dad.'

I wasn't sure I believed her. Veronica was always chasing a deal. They didn't always materialise.

'What are you talking about?'

'It's... a deal. Something I tried to put together a couple of years ago but it fell through. I might be able to get it together again.'

'What, like a development site? Is it a hotel?'

She smiled. 'Nothing like that. I'll tell you once it's all done. I'm close. You know how it goes, though. It's all about timing.'

I shake my head.

'Maya,' she said, turning to face me. 'I want to look after you.'

'That's sweet. But we'll be okay.' I smiled at her.

She shook her head, the expression on her face serious. 'I'm I love with you, Maya.'

It had taken a moment for her words to register, for me to entirely understand her meaning. It was both entirely unexpected but also incredibly right.

'Maya? Are you okay?' I've forgotten Liam is standing in front of me. My mind comes back to the supermarket. The reds and greens of the produce section are too bright, their colours glaring. This world feels too real.

'I loved her,' I say out loud. Liam looks at me as if I've said something strange, which I have. My internal thoughts have mixed up with my external world. It doesn't faze me anymore. 'Don't you miss her?'

He's confused but he answers anyway. 'I'm sad that she's gone. And I'm devastated for Max. But to be honest, Maya, she didn't want anything to with me over the last few years. Now her parents are keeping me from Max. I don't know what to do.'

I nod. 'That'll all be okay. Get a court order. DNA if you need. Kids need parents. Max needs you.' I'm not sure where the words come from but they ring true. I wonder what's going to happen to my own boys now.

Liam looks over his shoulder at something. He looks angry.

'Maya Henry?' A cold voice is calling my name.

I turn around and Stacey Collins is there, standing next to another officer who I haven't seen before.

'Maya?' she repeats, blinking. Her expression is serious.

There's a heavy hand on my shoulder, I flinch but it's only Liam. He steps between me and Stacey Collins.

'Maya, I'm requesting you to come with me to Waringal station for questioning.'

Liam puts a hand in front of me, shielding me from Stacey. 'Come on, don't you think we've all had enough of this? She's grieving. Let her be.'

Stacey glances at Liam but then turns to look me straight in the eyes. 'We'd like to question you in relation to the murder of Veronica Hayes.'

'You did,' I say. 'You already did.'

'Yes, I know. And this time we'd like you to come with us to the station. I don't want to arrest you or handcuff you. But the detectives on the case would like to speak with you.' She's speaking slowly now, like she thinks I'm a small child. Or psychotic.

'How long is this going to go on for? Give us all a break,' says Liam.

A small crowd has formed around us in the supermarket. One of the officers steps closer to me. A second is edging Liam away. For the first time, I notice there are more police. There's four of them just inside the glass automatic doors. Six cops in Cape Cross and it's not even New Year's Eve.

I feel hands on my shoulders. It's not Liam now, but Stacey and her colleague walking me out of the supermarket. Obliging, I go with them. It feels like everything is in slow motion. Like I'm drunk, or drugged or half asleep.

'I would never hurt Veronica,' I say but no one answers. 'I would never hurt her. I loved her.'

28

ISOBEL

'I don't believe any of this.' I shake my head, my eyes on my phone screen. I've been texting Maya all afternoon, ever since Liam called me. She hasn't answered. 'Maya doesn't have a violent bone in her body.'

It's close to dark outside and the pub is full, but Liam has someone covering for him on the floor. We're out the back in his office. It's a small room with a chunky pine desk in the middle and diplomas on the wall that look like they've been gathering dust for a decade.

The noise of the pub is muffled by the closed door. It's stuffy and about five degrees too warm, but I don't complain.

'You don't need to be a violent person to hurt somebody.' Liam has a cup of green tea in front of him, which makes me realise every other time we've been together we've both been drinking.

'What did she say exactly?'

He takes a moment to answer. 'We were talking about Max. About being a parent. Then all of a sudden the cops were there. I didn't notice them at first. I was angry when I saw them.'

'Angry? At Maya?' There's cup of black coffee in front of me but I haven't touched it.

'No.' He shakes his head. 'Stacey Collins. That detective. I told her to give us all a break. Then I clicked that this was serious. That Maya was in trouble. She was real strange, Isobel. She wasn't herself at all. She said that she loved Veronica.'

'They spent a lot of time together. Veronica was her best friend.'

'No, that's not what she meant. Not best friend. I think she was in love with her.'

'In love? Like in a relationship together?'

He nods. 'It sounded a lot like romantic love.'

Well, that was something else entirely. All signs pointed to Veronica having a lover. It had been on everyone's minds that love gone wrong led to someone pushing her off those cliffs. In my mind, that dark, hypothetical figure had always been a man. But Maya?

'Maya in love with Veronica...' I say the words out loud with a sigh. 'I didn't see that coming.'

We are both silent as the possibility sinks in.

'I guess it could make sense.' Liam is lost in his own thoughts, looking at the wall over my shoulder.

'People fall in love all the time. Why wouldn't it make sense?' I ask.

'What if Veronica wasn't in love with Maya?'

'Oh.' I bite my lip. Maya is gorgeous. I doubt she'd ever been rejected in her life. 'Maybe we shouldn't speculate.'

Liam laughs. 'Now you don't want to speculate? After two weeks of break-ins and conspiracy theories?'

I shrug. 'I don't want to speculate about my friend.'

'Well, if it was Maya then the police know. They probably always knew. It's solved. You can relax.'

'I went to yoga with her the other day,' I say, my coffee cup in hand. 'I don't think I could kill someone and then go to yoga.'

He shrugs. 'It doesn't all fit for me either. I agree with you, Maya's gentle. She would never hurt anybody. Not to mention, she's got kids to worry about.'

'Exactly.'

'But maybe it was the heat of the moment,' he adds.

'Maybe it was someone else,' I say.

'Maybe you want it to be someone else.'

I take a few moments to respond.

'It never takes long for news to spread around here. So, I guess we'll know soon,' I say.

'And in the meantime, things are back to normal,' he says. 'For us, at least.'

29

ISOBEL

Edmund Keane is sitting opposite me. We're alone in his office; he's already sent his staff home for the day. The deco is far from commercial, the table looks like an antique and the ornate timber chairs are over-stuffed and upholstered in teal velvet. There is a slight smell of tobacco in the air. I wonder if he smokes in here.

'The title to the house is in your name and it's unencumbered. There's never going to be any questions surrounding that.'

He has hit the ground running. Before I get the chance to ask a single question, he is firing information at me.

'This is about my house?' I ask.

He leans forward over the table that is between us. 'I was under the impression that you knew what was going on. When I spoke to Jennifer-'

'My mother?' I cut him off.

He hesitates. 'Yes… This is about your trust fund.'

The one I've been ignoring since my last birthday. He has a pile of paperwork in front of him and when I look closely, I can see my name on it. 'But you're not the administrator, it's looked after in Melbourne,' I say.

He shakes his head. 'That was all changed, not long before your Grandfather died. He asked me to look out for you. As a friend.'

'You were friends?' I thought there was conflict between them.

'Yes, we played golf together for thirty years. Jonathon never told you?' He stops for a moment, looking up from the paperwork.

'I thought you didn't get along.'

'I suppose we did have a few tiffs over the years… but nothing serious.' He gives a small smile.

I nod. 'I didn't know.'

'He was worried about the will being contested by other family members.'

'Mum wouldn't do that. She's respectful of her father's wishes. Even now, they won't take any money from me. They don't even like coming to the house.'

He tilts his head, looking at me through square framed

glasses.

'We need to be clear.' He pauses and shuffles his paperwork into a neat square. 'Isobel, when you say your parents, you're talking about Jennifer and Mateo Franco.'

'Of course.' Dread is pouring into my stomach.

'For the purpose of this conversation it would be better to refer to them using their names. Not mother or father.' He watches me carefully. 'Clarity is important right now.'

'Clarity? Around what?'

'You haven't spoken to Jennifer, have you?'

I shake my head for no. My head is running through blood types. O-negative and A-positive. And the truth that I can't belong in that family tree.

The truth sits inside of me like a heavy stone. 'They're not my parents.'

'You've found out recently?' he asks.

'Yes.'

He leans back, the chair beneath him squeaks. He lets out a gentle sigh. 'I'm sorry it's happened this way. My understanding was that Jennifer had explained the situation to you.'

It turns out my mother can keep a secret after all.

'I knew something was wrong. But I didn't know what it was. There are a lot of loose ends I can't tie together.'

'I don't know all the circumstances around your birth. That's not my role. I'm here to protect you now, in the present. Financially, that is. Legally.'

I nod.

'I'm sorry, Isobel. Jonathon has done everything possible to protect you.' He moves the paper in front of him again. Jonathon Esmore is not my real grandfather, I realise.

My family. My father too. It was hard to imagine that he had lied to me my whole life. Then I paused, Edmund Keane had talked about a change to the will.

'So, this is about my grandfather's will?'

'Yes. I've been wanting to speak with you about it for some time. Your grandfather was concerned that if word got out that you weren't his biological grandchild that someone would challenge his will at some point.'

'So, that's why he changed it. But he cut out his own daughter.' I sighed looking at the table in front of me. I didn't really care about the money. I would have been happier knowing the truth.

'We decided that would be the best option. His prerogative was to protect you. After he found out that you weren't Jennifer's biological daughter, he was very thorough. Not leaving money to any biological family makes it harder for other biological relations to contest the will.'

'My grandfather didn't always know? When did he find out?'

I had assumed that he was a part of whatever secrets were being kept from me.

'He found out six months before he passed. We met at the time and discussed options. We had to future-proof things, so to speak.' He was leaning forward again, engaged. 'That's what I need to discuss with you.'

'Future proofing?'

'Yes. Like I said, the house is untouchable. It was yours before your grandfather died, which is hard for anyone to dispute. However, there were parts of his original will that mentioned grandchildren. The newer version only names you-'

'So, he didn't care?'

'Sorry?' He looks confused and I don't think he likes being interrupted.

'He didn't care that I wasn't his granddaughter?'

Edmund smiled. I could tell it wasn't something he did often. 'He very much considered you his granddaughter. Otherwise I wouldn't be sitting with you right now.'

'Okay.' I feel myself relax a little. While it hurts that my family kept this secret from me, there's something amazing about the fact they still considered me their family. That they were all willing to fight for me.

'So, I can see you've had very little to do with this trust.' He raises his eyebrows as he waits for my reply.

'No. I wasn't able to touch it until recently. And, well if I'm honest, I don't have a mortgage and I've always made a decent wage. I haven't needed it.'

He nods. 'Well, it's there. And it would be prudent to pay it more attention, even if you don't mean to utilise it. Although, it could be configured to provide a monthly stipend.'

I knew how trusts worked. It could be configured to do anything. 'How much?'

'Well, if we ran the numbers conservatively you could draw twenty thousand a month. It would be up to you.'

'Twenty thousand?' I lean forward, my hands flat on the table. I knew there was money but I'd never so much as looked at the statements. I thought there might be thousands of dollars... not millions.

'Your grandfather cared a great deal about you. And... well it's not my place to get involved with this side of things. But if he was anything like me, he didn't tell you enough. He was proud of you. He thought you were a good person.'

'Thank you.' It sounds like it's not enough of a response. I know I should say something more but I can't think of what.

'I want you to be aware that we may face challenges. There may be people who try to contest the will or make a claim on the estate.'

'Like who?' I have no other family. There's only my parents and I know they would never do anything like that.

He opens his mouth to speak but then he closes it again.

'Who?' I repeat. He knows exactly who but he's not going to tell me.

'Let's worry about that when it happens. I only wanted you to be aware that it could come up. And in the meantime, think about whether you would like to change the structure of the trust to give yourself an income.'

'I'll think about it.'

He nods. 'Is there anything else?'

I go to tell him no, but then I remember one thing. 'The old hospital. You own the site, right?'

'Yes,' he says. Confusion washes over his face. 'I own it with my brother in law. I have for years. Something to leave for my own grandchildren.' At the mention of his grandchildren, a smile forms on his face.

'How well did you know Veronica Hayes?'

His face falls. 'Not well.'

'But you did know her? You managed a family trust for her.'

I don't know what I'm expecting him to say. I don't think he had anything to do with Veronica's death. Maya still hadn't answered my calls or messages and as far as I can tell she was is in police custody. I should have had all my answers. I should be able to let this go. But I can't. Something isn't right.

He nods. 'I did. She approached me about the hospital site.

She had a buyer for it. They'd had plans drawn up for the land.'

'Townhouses, right?'

'Yes,' he nods. 'The offer was good; the money was right. Like I said, I wanted to hold on to it. I've worked hard all my life; the money wouldn't change anything.'

So, when she tried to get Edmund Keane to sell the land, Veronica was met with resistance. If there's anything I've learned about her, it was that she didn't give up easily.

'And the trust?'

'She asked me to set it up about a year ago. Initially, I did. But then I found out there was a conflict of interest. I couldn't look after her anymore, so I passed her on to a colleague of mine in Melbourne to help.'

'What kind of a conflict?'

'I can't answer that, Isobel. Confidentiality. Just like I never answered her questions about you and your grandfather.'

30

MAYA

'If you had of been honest, this would have been a lot easier.' Stacey Collins sits opposite me. Her back is straight, her eyes alert, and she is recording everything I say.

I don't answer.

They asked their questions for over an hour. I answered every single one in a bold, flat voice like I had nothing to hide. I don't anymore. Thank goodness for location services on phones. My data backs up every word I've said.

'We will have a car take all of you home shortly.'

'All of us?'

'David and your two sons are here. Don't worry. There's a social worker with the boys and they're having a great time playing Nintendo.'

Stacey leaves, pulling the heavy door to the interview room

closed behind her. I assume it's locked, but I don't try it. I stay in my vinyl chair, awaiting directions. I think about David in another room just like this one. They'll be comparing our stories, looking for inconsistencies.

Love isn't binary. People say you fall out of love like you might fall out of bed. Love is different every day. Like a tree, it can bloom and flourish or it can die over the course of a long winter.

Something happened in those first few years with the twins. There was a change inside me. One day, and I don't know when it was or exactly what happened, but I loved him less. It was long before that night in the bar with Veronica. That was a symptom of a bigger problem. David and I started on a decent day by day, inch by inch, I loved him less. And then I met Veronica. I began to love her. More and more. I didn't know it was happening; it was so gradual.

The door squeals and Stacey Collins bursts back into the room. The small space plus the fact that I'm sitting down make her seem larger than life.

'Your husband's no talker,' she says.

'No.'

'He doesn't have an alibi for that night. He's saying he was with you. At home, watching a movie. But that can't be right, Maya. You told us you were with Veronica. Arguing out the front of her house.'

'Maybe he's got the nights mixed up. He was at home.'

'Was he?'

'He was at home when Veronica called me. Then I went to her house to take her laptop to her.'

'Which you ended up forgetting.'

'Yes.'

'And when you got back, where was he?'

We had been sleeping in separate rooms for months. The door to the master bedroom was closed. Our argument had upset me. I went into the bathroom, turned the shower on as hard as it went and cried for ten minutes. Afterwards, I slept the guest room. I never looked in on David. I assumed he had gone to bed.

'In bed,' I answer.

'And what, you got into bed with him?'

'We sleep in different rooms.' She nods. Something tells me she already knew that.

'Did you see him when you got back?'

'No.'

She nods.

'Does he take his phone with him when he goes out?' asks Stacey.

Always, I think. Anyone with kids does. I nod.

'And you do too, right?'

I nod again. She will get the phone records. They'll show exactly where everyone was that night.

'Did they get on, Maya? David and Veronica?'

'No.' There's no point in lying anymore.

'Did he ever do anything to make you think he could be violent?'

'Yes.'

'Maya, do you think your husband killed Veronica Hayes?'

'No.'

I never told him I wanted to leave, or Veronica's offer to move in with her. Let alone that she confessed her feelings to me. But he knew, somehow he knew. David always told me I was an easy person to read, that I should never play poker. He called it my lie face, a certain look that gave me away every time. I've never been sure what my tell is. He was careful to make sure he didn't give it away. Why would he want to lose that advantage?

For a few hours on a Saturday afternoon, I was going to leave my husband. Now I don't know if I'll ever be free of him. Veronica is gone. Some days, I feel like I'm not that far behind her. The day she told me she loved me was the last day she was alive. I never had time to say it back to her. She had less than fourteen hours to live.

31

ISOBEL

It's dark out, the few streetlights in the town have little effect. Once I'm away from the main street, my headlights are the only source of light. My mind is full like a rain cloud ready to burst as I navigate the short drive home from Edmund Keane's office.

A pop song plays on the radio. It's something old and catchy that was around when I was in high school. With annoyance, I flick the stereo off. I'm not just annoyed at the pop song.

A few years ago, I saw a documentary about people who found out later in life they were adopted. They were angry; they felt cheated. Children are better off when they know where they come from.

It's something that never occurred to me; that my parents might not be my parents. Honestly, I don't know how they pulled it off. I've seen myself in baby photos. Small and pink and puckered, I can tell that I'm a newborn. So wherever they got me from, they had me from day one.

And then there's my birth certificate. I've seen it, I was born in the same hospital that I broke into not that long ago. Both of their names are on it. That's not what happens in an adoption, right? It will always have your birth parents' names on it.

Why didn't they tell me? Did they think I was better off? That I would never notice because we look so similar? Maybe that's why they picked me. For a moment, I imagine them looking over a row of babies in their cribs. Looking for the one with the right hair, the right eyes. One they can pass off as their own.

That's the other thing. They told no one. They couldn't have. A secret like that would never stay a secret in Cape Cross. Even my grandfather didn't find out until the end of his life.

Nobody knew. I've seen photos of my mother pregnant. More than one, all from a time long before Photoshop. And if that baby wasn't me, who was it? A fake pregnancy? A baby she lost?

My parents are far from perfect, but they're not liars, they're not conspirators.

I figure there is only one way to find out. I've driven home by instinct, but that doesn't mean I have to stay here. They need to tell me the truth about everything, and they need to tell me tonight. As I pull the car back out of the driveway, my phone rings. The car's Bluetooth picks up the call and I see Liam's name on the screen in front of me.

'Hi,' I answer. The clock in the car says it's 7:13pm. 'Is every-thing okay?'

'Hey. I just saw Maya at the pub. The police have released her.' His voice is tense.

'Really? That's great. How is she?'

'Not good. She seemed really upset. David was with her. She might have been crying.'

'Is she still there?' The pub was only a ten-minute drive from my house.

'No, she left a few minutes ago. I tried to talk to her, but she seemed… well, I don't know. Something was going on, she was preoccupied.'

'Do you know anything else about the case? Have they charged her?'

'No. She could be out on bail for all I know. Everyone's talking about it and they've all got a different story.'

It had never rung true for me. Maya wasn't acting like someone who had killed their lover in a rage.

'Iz, are you all right?' I realised the line between us had been silent for more than a minute.

'Yeah. Just thinking.'

'Are you at home?'

'I'm parked in my driveway but I'm about to go talk to my parents. I found some more stuff out.' I take a breath. I don't want to relay it all now. 'You know, it's probably not so bad. Compared to what Maya would have been through today.'

'You want to talk later? I'll finish up here around ten.'

What I really wanted to do was talk to Maya and make sure she was okay. She hadn't returned my messages, I guess she didn't want to talk. It would be better to talk to her tomorrow. My anger at my parents was still there, simmering deep in my guts.

'Maybe. I've got to sort some stuff out first.'

I go to reverse out of my driveway, but something else catches my eye. There's someone standing at my front door.

32

ISOBEL

'You've got some nerve.'

The voice in the darkness startles me. I've left my car in the driveway and walked to my front door. The neighbours' windows are dark, none of them are likely to be at home.

'Heather?' I call out to Veronica's mother.

She's short, shorter than me and slim. Every other time I've seen her, she's been wearing a cardigan with a dress. Today she's in pants and a rain jacket.

'Of course it is,' she scolds.

I reach inside by handbag for my phone, pulling it out and unlocking it.

'I'll call the police if I need to,' I say. 'What do you want?'

The sensor lights I had installed haven't switched on and

we're both standing in the darkness. I have no idea what to do. Maybe I should run away. Heather isn't young, I'm guessing she's around sixty, much like my own mother. I could get away from her in a heartbeat if I needed to.

'What do you want?' I repeat.

She laughs and her eyes move away from mine. 'I want Veronica back.'

'Of course you do. Everyone does.' I don't really know what to say.

She laughs again and this time she shakes her head. 'No, they don't. Someone doesn't. They strangled her then pushed her over a cliff. You don't want her back, Isobel. She was getting in your way.'

Now I have even less of an idea what to say.

'You have no idea what the real world's like, do you, Isobel?'

I take a step backwards. It feels like maybe I should have followed my first instinct and got out of here. My car is not far and running on foot could be even faster.

'Do you want me to call someone to come get you?' I ask.

'You've got an education, don't you? I hear you've got a law degree and a career to go with it. This monstrosity of a house. And now I hear you've got a boyfriend too.'

A boyfriend. Is she talking about Liam?

'You know he was Veronica's boyfriend? And then you took him. And Maya. You took her friend.'

Her voice is laced with crazy. No moon, no stars, just me and a woman on the psychotic side of grief. 'Would you like me to call your husband? I'm sure he can come and get you.'

She rolls her eyes. 'That useless lump? I doubt it. Anyhow, I'd much rather stay here and talk to you. Why don't you invite me inside and show me your lovely house?'

'No.' I dial 000 on the phone and wait for the line to connect.

'No? You don't like sharing things. You enjoy taking them, though. Things that are Veronica's.'

'I didn't know Veronica. I never met her.'

'But you found her. You found her down there, all alone on the beach. Don't you think that's a little strange? You were there one to call the police. Now you're seeing her boyfriend. Spending time with her friends.'

'Heather, I'm calling the police, it's ringing. They will be here soon.' I actively step away from her as I talk, putting as much space as I can between us.

'You can do that. I'll just tell them you killed my daughter.'

There is something so much stronger than sadness I can see in her eyes. Her grief has morphed into anger. Her mind is full of terrible emotions all come to the surface, ready to make her do something crazy. I am about to be the target.

'That's not true.' My voice is quiet and I'm almost back on

the street out the front of my house. It's probably not the right thing to say. I don't think there is a right thing to say. Nothing can calm her down. Heather hasn't moved from my front door. She doesn't have a weapon that I can see. She's getting closer to me.

'Maybe you didn't push her off a cliff, but you forced her there. If it wasn't for you, she wouldn't have been there. Your existence pushed her there. Your luck. It should have been hers. She was more deserving.'

There's no sense to anything that she's saying.

'Don't walk away from me. Face up to what you have done.'

What I have done? At that moment, the street fills with light. Car headlights are winding up the cliff road and turn into my driveway. It's a good thing I wasn't standing there.

Heather Hayes blinks into the light for a few seconds and then shields her eyes.

There's a clunk of a car door opening and then Liam steps out. He pauses, looking from Heather to me. 'Is everything okay?'

'No,' I say.

He turns and looks me up and down, standing on the curb of the road. 'Are you hurt?'

'No. I'm calling the police.' I am, but the call's not connecting.

Her scowl turns into a frown and she tucks her hands into the pockets of her jacket. 'Forget it, I'm leaving.'

Walking straight past me, she walks two doors down and gets into a white four-wheel-drive. The same car that followed me recently. I'm still standing in the same spot when I notice Liam has walked over to me, his arm is around me.

'Seriously, are you all right?' he asks. 'What the hell was that?'

Heather starts her car, does an abrupt U-turn and screeches away down the cliff road. As the sound of the engine fades into the night, I wait out the front of the house. I don't turn to meet his eyes; I keep watching the car until I can't see it anymore.

'She's crazy. She thinks I killed Veronica.'

'I'm sorry I didn't get here sooner. Come on, where are your keys? Let's get you inside. We can call the police.' He places a soft hand on the small of my back and pushes me towards the front door.

'I don't want the police here,' I say.

'What do you want then? Whoever you need, whatever. I'll make it happen.'

'Thai food. Thai food and Netflix.'

33

ISOBEL

.

Each time I pass a room, I stop and turn the light on. Damn the electricity bill, I'm keeping this place lit up like it's Christmas from now on.

Liam is a few steps behind me. He gives the heavy front door a push and it closes with a thump. He follows me upstairs without saying a word.

I hurry, almost in a jog as I take the stairs two at a time. When I reach the kitchen, I open up a high cupboard and pull down a bottle of whisky. Briskly, I grab two glass tumblers and pour an inch in each.

'I thought you were a wine drinker?' he asks, his eyes on the bottle of whisky.

'Wine is for good days, whisky for bad ones.'

Liam stands on the other side of the granite bench top, his

eyebrows raise as he watches me. 'Are you sure you don't want the police involved? I can call them.'

'Why?' I ask. 'They did nothing last time.'

'Yeah, but Heather was trespassing. And threatening you.'

'Maybe we can order some food instead. That Thai place near the beach delivers, right?'

I avoid his eyes. Picking up both glasses, I walk over to the couch and place the drinks down on the coffee table. I sit in a huff on the couch.

'Sure. I can order on my phone.' He sits down beside me and picks up the glass. After a small sip, he places it back on the table. 'What do you like to eat?'

'Whatever. Not a whisky drinker?' I look at his glass.

He shakes his head.

'I should have asked. Want a beer?' I feel a flash of guilt. I've always been a bad host.

'No, I'm fine.'

I take a long sip of my drink.

Liam tilts his head towards me. 'I know you're shaken up, but make a report. If nothing else, at least it's on the record.'

'On the record?'

He turns his legs towards me, moving slightly on the couch. 'Well, if it wasn't Maya… there's still an open murder case.'

'You think I need to defend myself?'

'No. Not at all. What if Heather's threatening other people? What if she hurts someone?'

'You think Heather did it?' I ask.

'No. I think she's a mess because her daughter is dead. Maybe she will do something.'

I take another long sip. I'm usually slow with alcohol. 'Do you think she could hurt someone?'

'Possibly.'

I nod. 'I'll go down the station in the morning.'

'Call them now. Don't change your mind later.'

'Okay.' I lean forward to pull my phone out of the side pocket of my jacket.

I don't call the emergency 000 line or even the station. Stacey Collins gave me her mobile number the first time I met her. It goes to voicemail, like I was hoping it would. I leave a message. Liam leans back into the couch, looking relieved.

'You know what, I will have a beer,' he says.

'Good.' I stand and go over to the fridge, grabbing a cold amber bottle by its neck. 'I'll drink your whisky.'

I sit back down and pass him the beer; he pushes his own whisky glass in front of me. For a little while we drink in silence.

'You used to do this before. Back in the old days,' he says, breaking the silence.

'The old days?' I look over at him, but he's staring at the black screen of the television.

'The old days of you and me.'

I ignore his nostalgia. 'What exactly did I do?'

'You stonewall. Your face goes blank and you won't look at anyone. You avoid talking.'

'I talk all day at work.'

'You know what I mean. You never talk about yourself. Not about what's going on inside your head.'

I sigh. 'Yeah, you're not the first to complain.'

'It made it hard when we were together. I never really knew what was going on with you.'

'You weren't the greatest communicator either,' I say.

'There were things I needed to talk about,' he says.

'Like what?' I ask.

He shakes his head. 'I'm sorry. It was a long time ago.'

'Yeah, it was.'

'You know there's another way to work through things. One that's really helpful and constructive, not only for you but for the people around you who are trying to work out what the hell is wrong.' He tilts his head, waiting for me to respond.

'Therapy? I'm not a fan.'

'It's way cheaper than a shrink. All you have to do is tell the other person what's going on.'

'Going on?'

'Yeah, what's going on. In your life or in your head. And they might not have any answers. In fact, they probably won't. But you'll feel a lot better just for saying the words.'

I've had conversations like this before. 'I'm sorry. There wasn't a lot of talking in my house when I was growing up. Not about feelings.'

He nods, listening.

'My Dad… a lot of stuff happened to him when he was younger. He was political. He ended up imprisoned for a few months. But by imprisoned I mean locked in a basement where he was tortured.'

'That's terrible. Is he okay now?'

'He's… Dad. He deals with it in his own way. He never speaks a word of it to me. I've just put all the pieces of it together over the years. I think that's his way of dealing with it. Not sharing it.'

'Maybe he doesn't want to talk about it because he doesn't want to burden you. If someone tortured me, I'd never want my children to bare that.'

I nod. I think about Max Hayes. I'd seen plenty of photos of him over the last week or so, and I don't doubt that Liam is his father. He'll likely be dealing with Heather if he wants a part of Max's life.

I take a deep breath and turn around, facing Liam. Maybe it is time I talk a little more.

'What happened before... it scared me when Heather was here. I didn't know what she wanted or what she would do. For all I knew, she had a gun or something. As well as being scared, I'm angry and pissed off.'

'Pissed off? Because she came here?'

I nod. 'Yeah, but because of what she said. I know you didn't hear it. She said I stole things. That I don't deserve the things I have because I haven't earned them.'

'She's a madwoman.'

'Some of it is true. Not in how she said... it's like what they say, the people who get to you the most are the ones who hit your weak spots.' I take a breath. Now I had started, I might not stop. 'You know, I only got into law because my grandfather paid the fees up front. He knew someone at the university. My final score on its own was too low.'

He shrugs. 'You had a good score, I remember. You could have done a semester of something else and gotten a transfer. If you wanted it, you could have gotten it on your own.'

'Luck plays a part. I wouldn't have my career if someone hadn't paved the way. Or this house. I inherited it unencumbered; not even a mortgage. I feel... I feel like a fraud sometimes. Especially when I compare myself to someone like Veronica. She worked hard and built a business. She raised a child. I can't even do that.' My voice cracks and I can feel hot tears on my cheeks. I try to wipe them with the sleeve of my jacket.

'Stop giving yourself a hard time.' His voice is quiet. He leans over and tucks of lock of hair behind my ear, then wipes my eyes with the back of his hand. 'You didn't ask for any of it. You worked hard and got that degree. You've had a good career. People give you their work because you're good at what you do. And this house? You're the person who renovated it. And, it looks a million times better than when we were kids. Maybe you got a little lucky, but you've worked with it. You've made yourself a life.'

I nod and take a deep breath. I want to believe him.

'What did I do to make her so angry?' I ask. 'Does she think I killed Veronica?'

He looks surprised at my question. 'Heather? No. She's in a bad place. And you're the closest thing to her. You're standing in the way of a volcano about to erupt.'

'Do you think it was because I found the body?'

'Maybe you remind her of Veronica. You have the same hair colour.'

'There's plenty of other redheaded women in town she could have fixated on.'

'Grief does strange things to people. Neither of us can understand what she's going through.'

Liam takes the last swig of beer. He makes a good point. I'm at the bottom of my second glass. 'Refill?' he offers.

'Sure.'

He helps himself to another beer from the fridge and brings the whisky bottle over to the couch, topping up my glass before he sits down.

There's a buzz, letting us know someone is at the front door. Liam's phone makes a noise at the same time.

'Thai food's here, should I go down?' he asks.

'Yeah.'

While he is downstairs, I grab some plates and cutlery and take them to the coffee table. It feels like the kind of night to eat on the couch. Liam comes back with a plastic bag full of food containers.

'That's a lot,' I say.

'Sure is.'

Without asking, I serve us both, putting some of everything on one plate and handing it to him, and then doing the same for myself. We both sit on the couch, food on our laps.

'So you were in therapy?' I ask.

He grins, 'What gave it away.'

'Everything. You never used to speak like that.'

'I guess not,' he answers. 'I'm much happier now. And yes, I was in therapy. A lot of it.'

'Wow,' I try not to smirk as I bring a forkful of flat noodles to my mouth.

'There's nothing wrong with that,' he says.

'No. It's kind of surprising. You were driven. I can't imagine you needing help.'

He laughs out loud. 'Not at all. Think of me as a duck. It looks calm on the surface but there's a lot going on underneath... And that took its toll. I never learned how to deal with stress. When things got hard, I fell on bad habits. You see, I have this weakness.'

'I'm sorry, I didn't mean to make fun of you,' I say.

He shrugs. 'It's okay.'

'So, what were the bad habits then?'

'Mostly gambling,' he looks away from me.

'When we were together?' I cast my mind back and try to remember. All I can think of is a couple of bets on horse racing. Did I not notice?

'It started then. It wasn't a lot. The more hours I worked, the worse it got. And then I lost my son because of it.'

'How?' I ask.

'Now and then I'd get an investment tip from work. Usually a biotech company positioned to do well. I made a bit of cash.

Veronica caught wind and wanted in. I told her there was a startup, and that I could invest for her. She gave me twenty thousand dollars.'

'Wow. So, it didn't pan out?'

'No. It was real. I planned to. But... I didn't invest her money. I lost it. Gambling.'

'So, she ended things over that?'

'Yeah. Things hadn't been great. But then she stopped me seeing Max. I'd lost all her savings and that she needed the money for him. For his future. She said that when I paid her back, I could see him. That I didn't deserve to until then. I kind of agreed with her.'

'Are you okay now? You found help?'

'I did. It was a lot of hard work. I re-evaluated a lot of things. Two years later, I had her money.'

'And?'

'She still wouldn't let me see him. I'd moved back here then and got the job at the pub. When I got a lawyer, she threatened to tell the town about what I'd done, even said she would press charges against me.'

'Wow. That's awful. So, you moved back to try to see him?'

'Yes. I thought it was my best chance. But also, because it's really hard to gamble here. The closest poker machines are forty minutes away. I work at the top pub because there's no betting there.'

'I had no idea about any of this. I wish I could have helped you.'

'It's okay, Iz. I learned a lot through it all. I'm better because of it. I like my life now. I didn't like it before.'

'But you lost your son.' He flinches a little at my words.

'Maybe not. He's only six. He's still a kid. The last few weeks have been awful, but they've also been my best chance to get him back.'

34

ISOBEL

Liam slept on my couch last night, drifting off while we watched a comedy. There are plenty of spare bedrooms, but I didn't want to wake him. Instead, I covered him with a blanket and left him to rest.

This morning, I woke up early. I haven't been able to sit still. Energy is pulsing through me, and I feel like I could run ten kilometres without breaking into a sweat. Whether it's anger or anxiety, I'm not sure. I think I'm tired of being in the middle of this mess and not understanding what is happening. I'm going on a run.

As quietly as I can, I shower and get dressed. My running clothes are at the top of my drawer. My feet slip easily into my shoes. Before I let myself out of the house, I glance into the lounge room where Liam still sleeps.

A strange nostalgia twists in my stomach. This is what it was like with Ben, just a few months ago. I would look in on him one last time before I went out for a run. I don't know if that's what I want from Liam. Everything he told me last night is still fluid in my mind. The image of him I have held for many years is shifting.

I open the front door to the soft light of early morning. I expect to see Liam's car in the driveway, but not the familiar white van that's parked behind it. I see my father standing beside it.

'Dad?'

He's waiting for me, his hands in his pockets, the blank expression on his face giving nothing away.

'You've got a visitor?' he calls, motioning to Liam's car.

I nod as I walk towards him. 'How long have you been here?'

'Half an hour or so,' he shrugs. 'I didn't want to wake you up.'

'You could have. I'm always up early.' I wait for him to do something, to explain why he is here. He doesn't. 'What's going on?'

'We need to talk, Isobel. Let's go for a drive.'

He motions for me to follow, opening the passenger door for me. He gets in the other side, looks over and waits for me to put my seat belt on.

'Who's here with you?' he asks.

'A friend.' I look away from him.

'You won't tell me who?'

'No.' The words come out of my mouth, short and sharp. 'Dad, I think it's time you started telling me the truth. This can't be one sided anymore. I thought that was why you were here.'

He sighs and starts the engine.

'I'm worried about you,' he says, watching me closely.

'Worried? Don't you think I've been worried? I don't know what's happening. Ever since that morning on the beach, I cannot understand what is going on. All I know is that I'm in the middle of all of it. You've shut me out. You and Mum both. You know something.'

The van turns on to the winding cliff road. We don't head to town, instead we take the road towards the wilder part of the coast.

'I think there is a lot going on. You need to distance yourself. I can take you to Melbourne. Have a break for a few weeks.'

For the shortest of seconds, I think he could be right. And then I see what he is doing. He's deflecting, making it my fault, moving the focus to me and away from himself.

'This is not about me needing a break.'

'Then what?' His voice is calm, drawing my attention to how irate I am.

'Pull over,' I demand. He glances over and reads the serious expression of my face. 'Pull the van over.' I repeat myself.

He touches the brakes gently and slows down. One side of the road is sand dunes and scrub. On the other side is the granite of the cliffs and the sheer drop to the ocean. There's nowhere for him to stop.

'There's a car park ahead,' he says.

I know there is. It's the same car park that leads to the beach where I found Veronica.

'Okay.'

We reach the car park; he pulls in, the tyres crunching on gravel. I wait for the groan of the handbrake before I speak.

'Why is someone following me when I go running, Dad? Why am I getting notes in my bedroom? Heather Hayes turned up on my doorstep last night and blamed me for her daughter's death.'

'Did she?' He looks surprised at my last comment.

'What has Veronica got to do with you and Mum? What has she got to do with me?'

'I don't want you to worry about it, Isobel. I think we should get you out of this town. I'm taking you to Melbourne, today.'

'No. You're not. We're not resolving things like that anymore. You've been keeping things from me since I was a kid. It feels like you don't trust me. Or that I'm not important enough for the truth. And now I treat everyone in my life the way you both treat me. I can't build a life of my own because I don't know how to trust another person, I don't know how to have a real relationship.'

He sighs. 'I'm the parent. My job is to protect you. Not to burden you.'

'But you are burdening me, don't you see? I'm in a perpetual state of not knowing. I'm left alone, imagining the worst case scenario.'

He looks away from me. I can't read his expression. Is he self-conscious? Guilty?

'You don't want to know those parts, Isobel. All I ever wanted was to keep you safe. I never wanted you to bare the things I have.'

'What things?'

There's no response from him. He turns away from me. 'I know that terrible things happened to you. I can't imagine how they make you feel.'

His answer comes fast this time. 'Have you considered that people in pain deserve their feelings?'

'Of course you don't.' My gut drops fast. What has he done?

'How can you know that?' His tone is dismissive and hurtful. But I push.

'I don't know that, Dad. You don't tell me. And I can't be an outsider in my own family anymore.'

'Don't say that. Stop saying you're an outsider. You're loved more than you realise.'

'Not knowing is hurting me. Everything is hurting me right now.'

I see pain ignite in his eyes at my words. He leans back with all his weight against the car seat and takes a long inhale of air.

'Isobel, if I tell you, don't be angry after the fact.' He watches me, waiting for my answer.

'I won't,' I promise.

He hesitates, staring firmly ahead. 'You ask what you need to know, and I will answer.'

'Anything?'

'Yes, anything.'

'Okay.' Where do I start? I worry that I will only get so many questions in before he snaps shut again.

'Where did your scars come from?'

It's a small movement, but I notice that he grimaces. His shoulders jolt backwards and he blinks. It was not the question he was expecting. He starts to answer.

'I have to start at the beginning. Back when I was twenty years old, I was a student at a university in Santiago. My father was a pilot, in the Air Force.'

I nod, but this is news to me. My paternal grandparents have always been a mystery.

'There was a military coup in 1973.' This I know. Since I was a teenager, I'd studied Chile's history, albeit through YouTube and Wikipedia. 'My father didn't come home one day. I can't tell you why, I've spent most of my life trying to find out. Most likely, he supported the sitting government, not the military.'

'He disappeared,' I say.

He gives a solemn nod. 'A lot did in those years. We were afraid to contact the military or the police. We asked around quietly. People were getting taken off the streets. Others were leaving the country.'

'Was your mother political? Were you?'

'No. It was enough to be associated with someone who defected. Through loyalty to the government, my father decided our fate.'

'What happened to your mother?' I ask, dreading the worst.

'She died in 1976. Liver disease. But it changed my sister.'

The word sister cuts straight through my heart. 'You have siblings.' I'd assumed I was the only child of only children. A lonely point at the bottom of a narrow family tree.

He gives a grim nod. 'One older sister. She was a schoolteacher, five years older than me. When our mother was gone, she looked hard for our father. There was a lot of anger inside her. She brought attention to us.' For a moment he stops talking, his head tilted to one side. Then he speaks again. 'I made a plan to join the army. Find out from the inside. But she wouldn't have it, plus she said it was near to impossible. She was right, too. There was something inside of me, a fire.' He brings a curled fist to his chest. 'I needed to do something. There were other groups I could join. Socialist groups. I started hanging around with activists.'

I put the rest together in my head. 'And then they came for you.'

'No. They came for my sister first. She went to work one morning and never came home. A few days later, they pulled me off the street, put a hood over my head and threw me in a van. I was glad, because I thought they'd take me to her. But they took me west of Santiago, to a camp. I heard they took her south, but I never saw her again. I wish I could have done more to protect her. The camp in the South... it was one of the worst.'

'And then you were tortured. That's why you have the scars.'

He shakes his head. 'Good torture leaves no marks. They used electricity, water. The things that left the marks I barley remember. They were just the beatings.'

'I'm sorry that happened to you.' He gives a small nod in acknowledgement. 'What about your sister?'

'I don't know. I never found out. Buried with hundreds of others or left to float in the Pacific Ocean. I won't ever forgive myself. My anger drove my actions. Those actions led to her end.'

'What was her name?'

He pauses. 'Isobel. I named you after her. I've always thought you looked a little like her. When I held you as a baby, I promised to protect you. I wanted your world to be a safe place. And I want you to know that every decision that I've made has been to do that as best I can.'

The information flows through my brain as I pull the pieces of his history together. like frayed pieces of fabric.

'When you held me as a baby?' I question. 'But I can't look like her, can I?'

He's surprised, but there is recognition in his eyes. He knows exactly what I'm talking about.

'I know, Dad. I know blood can't relate us. Why? Did you adopt me? Steal me? Where did I come from?'

With a sigh, he pulls the car back out on to the quiet road. 'It's time to have a discussion with your mother. I thought if I could get you out of town, I could keep you safe. But I have a bigger problem.'

'What's that?'

'I can't protect you both anymore.'

35

MAYA

The police let David walk free. I find him at the pub.

It's been hours since I left the station. I've picked up the boys, washed them, fed them and dropped them at my Dad's place.

'Are you sure you should spend time with David?' he'd asked.

Honesty is my new policy. This afternoon I filled Dad in on everything that has happened in the last few weeks. Most importantly, I'd asked him if I could take him up on his offer of moving in with him for a while.

'Of course you can,' he'd agreed without hesitation.

Stacey Collins called my mobile and told me David was out. Her tone implied a warning.

'Did he do it?' I asked.

Stacey hesitated. 'It's likely he'll be cleared. I can't say any more than that. Look after yourself, Maya.'

The call ended as abruptly as it had started.

He's long left the police station and he's not at home either. I find him, third attempt, hunched over the bar at the top pub, a full pint perched in front of him. I take the stool next to his, he barely looks up at me.

'How did you know I was here?' he asks.

'It wasn't that hard.'

'So, what is it? You came to ask for a divorce?' He takes a sip of his beer, still avoiding my eyes.

'I'm moving in with Dad,' I say.

'What about the boys?' He looks over at me now.

'We can work something out. But we need to talk about things first.'

'Which things?' he asks.

'We need to talk about Veronica. I need to know if you left the house that night.'

He leans back an inch in his chair and straightens his shoulders. 'I've already told my story to the cops. And they're the ones I have to answer to. Not you.'

I expected anger, not hostility. I realise that his anger was only threat, a tool to make me behave the way he wanted. Now I was moving out. He had no use for it. He would find more effective methods to suit his agenda.

'I have to trust you, David. If I leave those boys with you ever again, I need to know that they are safe. I can't do that until I know what happened.'

'Yes then. I left the house.' He looks over his shoulder. A few people are looking over our way. None of them are close enough to hear. I don't care anymore, anyway.

'And?'

'I left the house because you didn't pick up the phone. You ignored my texts.' That was true. I was too stressed from arguing with Veronica to answer them. 'So I went around to Veronica's.'

'Why?' I ask, genuinely perplexed.

'To catch you out. To know for sure what you were doing. I was tired of suspecting you. For a while, I didn't want to know. I wanted things to work out. But every day, Maya. Every day, you slipped a little further away from me than the day before.'

'That's not true.' I want to tell him it was him pushing me away. Maybe I am guilty too.

'It is. So were you, Maya? Were you having an affair with her?'

'No,' I say.

He scoffs. 'Veronica says you were. She said I wasn't enough for you, never was. That you were going to move into her house. That you loved each other.'

'She said I loved her?' Something lifted inside of me. I'd never told her. Maybe she knew.

David sneers. 'So, it's true?'

'We didn't have an affair. She asked me to move in, I never gave her an answer. There was nothing physical, David. Believe me, I have nothing to gain by lying.'

He nods, breaking his gaze away from me. It's hard to tell if he believes me. That's up to him, though. I'm not going to argue over it. There are more important things.

'Did you hurt her?' I ask.

'I didn't lay a finger on her.' His voice is steady. He's telling the truth.

'What did you do then? Why did you keep it a secret you were at her house?'

'I went there, I knocked on the door. I thought you were in there, maybe you'd hidden your car or something. Veronica came to the door. Told me to piss off, basically. So I just asked her outright what was going on.'

And it sounded like Veronica gave him the exaggerated version. She hadn't lied to David, but she had stretched things.

'I said some things after that. I made her angry.'

'What did you say?'

He takes a deep breath. 'That I might not be enough, but that she was less. She was all front and no substance, and I'd thought it since the moment I met her. I told her she was trying too hard because she would never be the person she liked other people to think she was. She could never be what you thought she was.'

What did she want me to think she was? I always thought of our relationship as honest. I knew she could put pressure on people, and that she knew how to manipulate. But she never did that to me. Did she?

'And then what?'

'She laughed at me. She was angry, but she laughed at me. She said that she would fix all that tonight and some things were about to change.'

'Change,' I repeated. I thought about our conversation in the park. Isn't that what she said then? That she had a big deal coming that would make things happen for us?

'What did you say?'

'Nothing,' he said. 'I didn't say another word. I went home. I saw her get in her car as I left.'

He'd fought with her only hours before she had died. That night, he'd never spoken to me. He'd gone to bed alone, steaming in his silent anger. The next morning he'd gone off to work without a word to me. Before he came home again, he'd have gotten word she was dead. No wonder he was so shaken in the days afterwards.

It feels like he is telling me the truth, but there is still a huge unanswered question. If David didn't hurt her, who else is there? How was she going to fix things? Where did she go that night after I went home?

36

ISOBEL

I bang on the door of my parent's house as hard as I can.

'Mum!' I yell. 'Open the door!'

Dad locks the van and walks up the path behind me. 'Calm down, Isobel. I've got a key. She doesn't move fast.'

My knuckles hurt from knocking. I take a step back and shake my hand. There's no sound inside the house, only the muffled sound of the dog barking in the backyard. I knock again, even louder. Dad nudges me out of the way with his shoulder, slipping the key into the lock. The door opens with a creak.

My mother stands in the entry, she's been a metre from the door the whole time I was knocking. Her expression is pinched and her mouth a flat line.

'Why didn't you open the door?' I ask.

She doesn't answer, she only looks at my father and me.

'Jennifer? Are you all right?' my father asks, his voice deep with concern.

'Mum, I need to talk to you,' I step inside the entry, but she pushes me back with a flat palm.

'Not now. Go home, Isobel.' Her eyes bulge. Is she angry? God, if anyone deserves to be angry, it's me.

I step back onto the concrete porch, but only out of shock. 'What?'

'Go home, now,' she repeats herself. It's the sternest she's spoken to me since I was a child. 'I need to be alone right now. You can both go.'

I hesitate a moment. I almost obey. But then anger takes over me again, snapping back into place like a rubber band. 'No. You need to answer my questions. Both of you.' I look at my father, his brow is crinkled with confusion.

Pushing past her, I step into the entry. Her hands push outwards, physically trying to stop me from coming inside.

'This has gone on long enough, you need to tell me the truth, Mum!'

It's the dated wall of mirror tiles that decides my fate. If it wasn't for them, Mum might have pushed me back out to the doorstep. Dad and I might have left. I don't know why, but I look at the reflection of the lounge room on the tiles. Standing just past the open sliding door between the entry and the lounge room is Heather Hayes.

She's holding a gun.

When I see the look in her eyes, I know things are bad. With both fists, I grab the fabric of my mother's shirt and try to pull both of us backwards out of the door. It's too late.

'Stop,' says Heather. 'Or one of you will get shot.'

Both her hands are on the grip of the gun, its short barrel is pointed at the ground. Her expression is livid. Her mouth is in a scowl and her skin is flushed.

'Well, she's coming inside now,' says Heather. 'All three of you, inside and sit on the couch.'

She takes a step back so she's against the front window. Someone has pulled the curtains shut. Raising the gun, she points it upwards at the roof while we file past her. My mother sits down on the couch, and I drop next to her. Searching her face for an explanation, I find nothing. Always calm, my father walks behind me and sits on my other side.

'You almost got a free pass, Isobel. Again,' says Heather.

'What's going on?' I ask, my voice low.

'Heather came over for a chat,' my mother replies, her tone flat.

'A casual chat with a handgun?' I ask.

'That's enough,' Heather snaps from the other side of the room. She's locked the front door from the inside. Maybe I should have taken my chances a moment ago and run for it.

'It probably won't be as bad,' says Heather, standing over us.

'What won't?' I ask.

I feel my mother nudge me in the side. I think she wants me to shut up. Heather paces back and forth in front of us. She's so angry she's frothing at the mouth. She was mad last night, but now she's reached a whole new level of insane.

'Death by shooting. It'll be over quickly. Not like strangulation. That takes a while, you know.'

'Heather, why are you here? Why do you have a gun?'

'I came over for a chat, Isobel. I wanted to ask your parents about a few things.'

'Maybe…' I start, and I don't know if I'm pushing her too far. 'Maybe you could put the gun down. It might be easier for us to talk.'

Heather stops pacing. She looks at me dead on. 'My God, Isobel. You really are annoying.'

'What?'

'Can you just shut up for once in your life? Can you just imagine, even if only for a moment, that you are not the centre of the universe?'

She turns towards me and points the gun at the centre of my chest. If she shoots me, the bullet will tear through my heart. I swallow hard.

I say nothing.

'That's better. Okay. Moving on. Jennifer, do you want to tell your daughter what you did?'

Heather looks at my mother. She turns the gun towards her, waiting for her answer.

'Mum? What's she talking about?' I say.

'Tell Isobel what you did so she could stay the star of her perfect fucking world. Tell her,' says Heather.

My mother looks downwards in her lap.

Through the white lace I can see the street. I make a silent prayer that someone walks by and notices that something is wrong. Anyone.

'You annoyed me when you turned up in town, Isobel. It's like you waited for Veronica to die, then you swooped in and stole her life.'

'I didn't know her. You know that.'

She ignores me. 'Like you didn't already have enough. The moment her body was cold, you moved in. Like a psychopath. I always thought people like that are born. It's genetic. You're proof that theory is wrong. You learned, surrounded by a family of people as bad as the adult you grew up to be.'

'What?' I look from my mother to Heather. My mother drops her head to her hands.

'I know all about you,' she directs her gaze at my father. 'I know you're some kind of war criminal. Running from your own country and hiding out on the other side of the world.'

'He's not a war criminal!' I shout.

'Oh, shut up, Isobel. Do I need to gag you? Say what you want about Veronica, but she knew when to be quiet.'

Heather paces back and forth in front of the couch.

'My Veronica was smart. I brought her up the right way. I taught her to work hard. To treat people right.'

I think Heather Hayes is verifiably insane and needs hospitalisation. She's not making sense anymore.

'I wonder how old you were when it happened. Two days? Three days? We'll never know. Veronica found some nurses from the old hospital. One of them told her that sometimes the babies' wristbands fell off when they bathed them. That's what she thinks happened. The most likely explanation. What are the odds of that?'

I stay quiet. My brain ticks over. I sit on the sunken couch, my shoulders square, as a million little pieces fall into place.

'You know why the wristbands fell off? Someone ordered the wrong size! The wrong fucking size. They were too big for babies. But instead of ordering another box, they did them up tightly. Budget restrictions.'

I pictured a tiny baby, maybe a few days old. Her wristband slips off in the warm water. Maybe the nurse who's bathing her notices, maybe she doesn't. They were always understaffed.

Two baby girls get taken back to the nursery. Both wrapped

up in soft white towels. Both pink-skinned, a small crop of crimson hair and those steel-coloured baby eyes that aren't really a colour yet. Each ends up in the other's crib. And each goes home with the other's family.

One of them grew up poor. The other got a trust fund. One worked hard and sunk her teeth viciously into every opportunity. The other...

'You didn't know?' Heather has been watching my face carefully this whole time. 'You had no idea. You really do live in a perfect world, Isobel.'

I look at my mother. She raises her head slightly and looks me in the eyes.

'How long have you known, Mum?' I ask.

'Just after the doctor diagnosed me. Two years ago. I already knew your father's blood type. He makes that joke.'

'Two types of blood.' I state.

She nods. 'I remembered your blood type from when you broke your arm. I looked it up online, what it meant. I never said a word to anyone. Not even your father. I could never work out what happened, not until Veronica turned up. I didn't really want to know.'

'It was you, in my house? Opening the filing cabinet? Leaving notes?'

She nods. 'I just wanted to keep you away from it all.'

'You could have told me the truth,' my voice is almost a whisper.

'Yes. She could have. Two years ago. We could have sorted it out with counsellors and tearful reunions. But she didn't. Have you worked out why, Isobel?'

'Why did you keep it a secret?' I ask. My mother has turned away from me. It feels like she's disconnecting herself from everything that is happening.

Heather leans forward so her face is right next to mine. 'Because of the money, Isobel. It's always about the money. She didn't want anyone touching your trust account.'

My mother is silent.

'Well, it's not your money, Isobel. Is it? You should never have been the one to inherit it. It should have been Veronica's. All she wanted was for you to share some of it. Which is fair. Generous, I think.'

But what about Veronica? She must have found out too. She wasn't trying to sell the hospital or do a deal. Well, maybe she was at the start. She talked to Edmund Keane. But she must have found something else in that storage room.

Perhaps it was the paperwork around her birth. Then she found the doctors and nurses who were there when she was born.

And when she said my grandfather stitched her up. That wasn't over the quarry or the hospital or some other piece of property. She was talking about herself. The inheritance that should have been hers. Veronica was never looking for a family, she was looking for a payday. She went straight to my grandfather. And when he died, she thought my mother inherited the money. She started on her.

I look at my mother. 'She approached you, didn't she, Mum?'

Veronica had been fighting my grandfather through the last year of his life, trying to get a piece of his fortune. It was almost laughable. If she had asked him for a chat and a coffee... well, he might have left something to her. But to blackmail him... there was nothing he would have hated more. A stubborn man and proud, he would have moved mountains to stop her getting a single cent.

For the first time, I realised he wasn't trying to keep my mother out of his will. He was trying to keep Veronica out of it. A will that left his own daughter out was harder to contest than one that was divided between family members. It wasn't pride that stopped my parents from taking any money when I offered it; they were protecting me.

'Not until after your grandfather passed,' she confirms. 'Veronica turned up on the doorstep.'

'She blackmailed you?'

'She would have if I had any money. Veronica didn't know that everything had gone to you.'

'How long have you known she was your daughter?'

My mother looks me in the eyes. She takes my hand. 'She's not my daughter. You are.'

'Hey!' Heather cries, stamping a foot on the floor. 'Veronica's not on trial here. Your mother is. So let's hear the rest of the story, Jennifer. What happened when Veronica knocked on your door?'

'Mum? Do you know what happened to her?' I whisper. I think I already know the answer.

She bit her lip, and fresh tears ran down her face. She looks to me and not to Heather.

'I'm so sorry, honey.' My mother wraps her arms around me. 'It was an accident. I was alone and it was late. She just kept asking questions... she was angry... I wanted her to stop. She said she had found a way to take everything. That the lot would be hers. The house and money in trust. She said I could give her half now or she would take all of it later and ruin you.'

'It's only money, Mum.'

'She told me you didn't deserve any of it. That she knew things about you.'

I nod. 'We had a couple of friends in common. She had been asking about me.'

'She told me that your grandfather bribed you into university. That you wouldn't be able to practise law. That you and Ben were running a scam at the tax office.'

'What!' Tax fraud! Well, give Veronica points for creativity. 'None of that is true, Mum. I paid full fees at university, but that's allowed. No one cares about that. Ben's an accountant, not a criminal.'

'I was afraid. And then I felt angry. Her handbag was open, on the floor right where your feet are now. There was a charger on top. A computer charger. I didn't want her to die, I wanted her to stop talking.'

'Mum…' My mother, who limps around most of the time and couldn't manage to bring in the grocery bags on her own had killed someone. It gives proof to the theory that anyone is capable of murder. In the right circumstances. With the right computer charger.

'Dad?' I look over at my father. 'Did you know?'

'I'm sorry, Isobel. She was dead when I got home. There was nothing I could do for her. What I did next was to protect you. Both of you.' He looks over to my mother.

The van in the car park. It was his.

'I'm sorry too,' my mother said.

Heather sighs heavily. 'You could have confessed to the police weeks ago and Isobel would have lived through this.'

My mother looks up at Heather. 'What?'

'You killed my daughter, Jennifer. It's only fair that I kill yours.'

Terror blooms deep in my guts as the understanding of her words hits me. It ripples through my whole body like a sick wave of nausea.

'No!' My mother shouts and tries to put her own body in front of mine.

'I deserve payback. You stole my daughter. You took a life.'

Then something amazing happens. Through those tired lace curtains, I see a blue and red light flashing in the driveway. Black shadowy figures dash across the lawn. Never have I been more grateful of justice only being a concept.

'Wait,' I say. With her back to the window, Heather has no clue that the police are outside.

She sneers. 'Wait? I've waited long enough.'

'No. There's something I need to tell you. Something about Veronica.'

The gun is pointed square at my chest again, her eyes widen as she waits for me to speak. I'm buying time. But then a truth hits me. And I think I should talk. Like Liam says.

'I didn't steal what she was born into. Not by intention. But she took it upon herself to try to steal it back. She determined her own fate.'

Heather is outraged and I think she's going to actually shoot me. But it doesn't matter, because at that moment, half a dozen armed police officers barge through the front door.

37

ISOBEL

It's been ten days since the police arrested my mother for murder. And yes, I still call her my mother and I always will. She kept an awful secret that led her to do an awful thing. It makes little sense to me that someone would take another life for the sake of money.

'How could you not know the baby you were holding wasn't your own?' Maya says to me. She pulls her hair up into a twist on the top of her head as she looks over to the swings. Noah and Jacob fly backwards and forwards. 'I could tell those two boys from each other the day they were born, and they're identical twins.'

There's a playground right next to the ocean. Tall pine trees shade it through the summer, and it's a popular spot. But today, early and on a weekday, we have it to ourselves.

I haven't been able to speak to my mother, but my father was released on bail. He's facing charges too; accessory after the fact. He never knew I wasn't his. Not until the night Veronica died.

How my mother killed a woman is baffling. It must have taken every ounce of strength she had, mentally and physically.

She is remorseful, so her lawyer tells me. And while she didn't surrender the night of the crime, she confessed and has assisted police ever since. That should impact her sentencing.

Heather has been charged as well. Stalking, conduct endangering life, use of a firearm with criminal intent... it's a long list, but in comparison to murder, they're minor charges. The max is ten years, but in the current system she'll only see two or three. If any. After all, she has a sympathetic case. Her daughter was murdered.

I had to get a new phone only a day after my mother was arrested. It rang so much I couldn't answer. Journalists from all over the country had gotten wind of the story. It made me nauseous to talk to any of them so I went to the nearest shop and got a whole new phone and number. It only took another twenty-four hours for them to find that one. I turned it off and dropped off the grid for a week.

I stayed home, eating Thai delivery and waited for the worst of it to blow over. Whenever someone knocked on the door, I ignored it. I was smart enough to stay away from the news websites. After weeks of desperately seeking the truth, I wanted it to give me a break.

A few days ago, I re-emerged. I turned my phone on. The first person I called was Maya.

We met here at the playground. Maya brings me coffee and remembers how I like it, which is nice. Her twins are in tow, they're loud and energetic and blissfully oblivious to everything that has happened around them.

'Have you seen Liam?' she asks.

'No,' I answer. 'But I spoke to him on the phone. He has full custody of Max now.'

There was no court battle or DNA testing. His birth certificate was retrieved from the registry and it named him as a father. Anyhow, with Heather in custody there was no one else to take him. Veronica's stepfather said it wasn't his responsibility since they weren't biologically related. Which is kind of ironic, given everything else that has happened.

It was Liam who saved my life that afternoon. He woke up that morning, cramped and uncomfortable on my couch. Not trusting my state of mind, he'd tried to find me. He tried the town and the beach and even Maya's house.

When he got to my parents' place I was already inside. By a stroke of luck, he didn't knock on the front door. Something stopped him; he saw a flash of Heather holding the gun in her hands through a gap in the curtains.

I saw him standing in the middle of the road, after the police stormed the house and got us out. He was yelling out to me from the other side of a hastily erected police barricade. It was impossible to hear him. All I could do was wave as the doors of an ambulance closed with me inside.

Maya watches her two boys on the playground.

'Does it help?' I ask. 'Knowing what happened that night?'

'Yes. But no. I miss her.'

I've never told her my mother's side of the story. I'm guessing that she reads the news and has a pretty good idea of what happened.

'Veronica wasn't a perfect person,' says Maya as if she's reading my mind. 'But I still loved her.'

I nod. 'Neither is Mum. But we don't love the people in our lives for their perfection. We love them as they are.'

'I left David,' she says, her eyes still watching the two boys navigating the slide. They climb up the wrong way, as if that's a lot more fun than going downwards, and then laugh when they make it all the way to the top.

'Did he know about Veronica?'

'He worked it out. I think he guessed what was happening before I did. It wasn't physical between Veronica and me. I can't define it.'

'Did he move out?'

'No,' she answers. 'I did. I moved in with my Dad. It's good for him to have an extra person around. Plus, these two.' She nods in the direction of the playground. 'What about you? What are you going to do now?'

I shrug and I honestly don't know. The law has lost its shine and I have no interest in my own business anymore. I still have the house, but there's not a lot else to keep me here. My parents might not even be around.

'Liam wants to see you. He's trying to give you some space.'

'Yeah,' I sigh. I'd figured that one out.

'He's one of the good guys,' she adds. But I already knew that.

ISOBEL - ONE MONTH LATER

On a café table opposite me, Max Hayes cuts his pancakes into small, square-shaped bites. He makes sure each piece has a little ice cream on it before he brings the fork up to his mouth.

Liam sits beside him. Neither of us adults are game for the sugar-laden pancakes. I've ordered eggs and a black coffee and Liam has toast on the table in front of him. The café is busy with both tourists and locals. Outside, it's a beautiful Sunday. Summer is in full swing, and Christmas isn't far away.

We've done this for the last three weekends. It's a little difficult to date a guy with a kid. Liam says that Maya has offered to babysit, even have Max once a week to help him out. Liam won't have it; he hasn't let Max out of his sight unless it's for school. He's taken an extended break from his job and said he was up to his eyeballs in holiday leave, anyway.

Max and Liam knock on my door at eight o'clock every Sunday morning. We head out for breakfast and later to the beach or the park.

I've never heard Max complain about anything. He's a sweet kid, he's softly spoken, and he thinks about things a lot. He's a lot like my father.

My father now has a grandchild. Or a biological grandchild, at least. I'm not sure if it means something to him. He will never be a great talker. I can understand where he is coming from. I'm not ready to talk about the fact that my real mother and my biological mother are both in prison.

After we've finished and paid the bill, we walk down the Main Street towards Safety Beach. The sun is beating down hot and it's warm enough to swim. Families are dotted along the sand, towels and beach umbrellas marking their places. It's so close to my home, but this is a completely different piece of coastline.

'Can we swim?' Max grabs my hand. He does this whenever we walk somewhere. I wonder how big the hole in his heart is. I nod and he grabs Liam with his other hand and leads the two of us down the hill. Liam looks across the top of Max's head and smiles at me.

Max is one of those kids that needs to be shown love all the time. He likes to stay close to me and always hugs me good-bye. I may never have a child of my own, but right beside me are a man and child waiting for me to love them. I hear

Heather Hayes' voice in my head, calling me a thief. A stealer of lives.

Guilt twists my stomach at the thought this life could have been Veronica's. I chase it away. She was a good mother to Max, but she spent every other moment chasing money. And eventually she chased hard enough that she met her own end.

We reach the sand; I step out of my sandals and then pick them up off the ground. The crisp sea wind is cool against my skin. Max runs ahead, keen to see if the water is warm. Liam stops and waits for me. He slips his arm around my waist as we walk towards the still sea. It's an aqua colour today, its hues shining brighter as the weather warms each day.

'You know, we will have to go on a proper date one of these days,' he says. 'I could take Maya up on her offer to babysit.'

I wonder if we should wait. Maybe Max needs more time to adjust. I should decide what I will do for work. But if I've learned anything, it's that things are rarely normal. If you wait for the right timing, it will never happen.

'Okay,' I answer. 'That sounds nice.'

Our births are a terrible lottery. The people you are surrounded by will shape you, for better or for worse. An act of chance can change your future at any moment. None of us know what might be ahead. But I can see what's in front of me right now. And that's enough.

ACKNOWLEDGMENTS

Thanks to you, the reader, for reaching the end of this book. It means a lot to me that you chose this story, either off a screen or shelf, and joined me for this journey.

If you'd like to know about new released, giveaways and sales, you can join my mailing list here. If you would like to get in touch you can do this at reneekirabooks.com.

Don't worry, I write slowly and never spam or share an email, so I won't flood your inbox.

Thank you to all of the people who helped me along the way with this book. Thanks to my husband, Daniel and my mother, Janeen who were my earliest readers.

Thanks to Traci Finlay for her brilliant beta reading skills and to Ash Spring for her incredibly precise proofreading.

See you next time.

Renee.